Heartbeats:
Voices Against Oppression

Edited by Jax Goss

Heartbeats: Voices Against Oppression
ISBN: 978-0692230749
Cover Design © Luke Spooner
(www.carrionhouse.com)
Published in partnership with M. Kate Allen, Fey
Publishing, and Solarwyrm Press.

DEDICATION

To anyone who's ever had their freedom threatened or stolen from them, this book is for you.

This book is also dedicated to everyone who fights to make the world a freer, safer, and more just place for all of humankind.

TABLE OF CONTENTS

INTRODUCTION

The news about over two-hundred Nigerian girls having been kidnapped came to me in a Facebook post by Melissa Atkins Wardy, owner of pigtailpals.com and an advocate for changing the way people think about childhood and gender roles. Ms. Wardy was flabbergasted that this kidnapping, having happened two weeks prior, had received so little attention from news outlets and in social media. Her Facebook post pointed to her own blog post with details culled together about the kidnapping along with links to resources that would allow her many readers to speak up and help out.

I wept at the news about these young women. I was appalled at myself for my ignorance about their kidnapping, and furious at others who had heard the news and minimised or dismissed it. Boko Haram, the religious terrorist group that committed the kidnapping, was culpable for this horrific evil; but in this age of global news, as a middle-class American sitting at her kitchen table, browsing the internet in complete freedom, I felt my own brand of responsibility —responsibility not for what had happened, but responsibility to help undo it with whatever resources I could muster. Ms. Wardy's post was an invitation to choose to speak rather than to be silent, and I found myself wondering what I could possibly do beyond engaging in mere slacktivism.

Here's the thing: I'm not independently wealthy. I don't lead an army. What could I do?

Write.

My ever-persistent muse reminded me that whenever I have felt the effects of marginalisation, I have responded with the greatest power I have: my writing voice. And when my own power isn't enough, I call on others with powerful voices to join me.

The seedling idea for an anthology called to mind two dear writer friends of mine who are independent publishers. Kristen Duvall of Fey Publishing and Jax Goss of Solarwyrm Press are women I trust, women who know what it means to be daring and prophetic in both writing and publishing. When I went to them with my idea, they each expressed interest without hesitation. Thus *Heartbeats: Voices Against Oppression* was conceived. We would announce a call for submissions on our respective websites and social media outlets inviting writers to submit short stories that addressed enslaving and enslavement. All contributors would do so without compensation, allowing us to direct all proceeds to a non-profit anti-human-trafficking organisation called the Not For Sale Campaign, which seeks to uncover, put a stop to, and prevent modern slavery.

The stories contained in this anthology are laden with enormous power—the power of the oppressor and the power of the oppressed. We hope that in reading these stories, your heart will be stirred into a great cry for freedom, and we hope that our voices, when joined together, will raze all fortresses of oppression to the ground.

M. Kate Allen
May 2014

THE TREE OF KNOWLEDGE

BY M. KATE ALLEN

It all began with God.

I was walking along one day, minding my own business, when I came across one of those street preachers. He was holding up a sign that said, "God hates fags". I, being the good Christian girl I was, nodded my approval, hoping he would nod his approval at my approval. He smiled with gleaming teeth, straight and pale and perfect, and I knew then that he knew something I didn't.

"What's your name?" he said, his teeth sparkling in the midday sun.

"Ellie," I said.

"Elaine?" he asked.

"Yes, but I prefer Ellie," I said.

Lines of muscle rippled beneath his pressed khakis as he shifted his weight forward. "No, Elaine, God gave you a name, and if you want to honour God, you must embrace that name with all your heart."

He bent to set down his sign, his thirty-something body rippling again. He was tan, but not too tan. His dark brown hair matched his eyes. His white polo bespoke something ethereal—rich, blessed, pure. I could sense something in him as he rose. He moved a step closer and I caught a whiff of something. Old Spice? His clean-shaven face revealed an earnestness I often felt in my search for... well, God, I suppose. But it wasn't really a search if God was all around. Obviously.

"Have you read the Bible?" he asked.

Heat entered my cheeks and bloomed on my chest just above my sun-dress. "Not all of it," I admitted.

"This is the day the Lord has made, Elaine—God intended for us to meet so you could know him and be saved." He picked up his sign, linked my arm through his, and I imagined that this stranger had been destined to become my own personal companion on the journey to Emmaus, where we would meet the Risen One.

ooOOoo

"Look at me!" he says in a low voice. He doesn't use my name anymore. I lift up my eyes, which are filled with tears of conversion. "Now say it again!"

"I will love the Lord my God with all my heart, and all my soul, and all my strength."

"That's right," he whispers. "Again."

"I will love the Lord my God with all my heart, and all my soul, and all my strength," I say, feeling the pulse of his breath with each phrase.

"Again!"

"I will love the Lord my God with all my heart, and all my soul, and all my strength," I whisper, and he cries out to God with joy. My converted heart is his manna from God. He can hardly get enough.

One day, after preparing himself meticulously in the shiny mirror that only he is allowed to use, he goes out on one of his usual preaching missions to save souls. It's been eight months since he saved mine, and this is the first time he's leaving me in charge of the mansion. He's given me careful instructions not to go near the tree of knowledge, because if I eat of its fruit like wicked Mother Eve, I will be damned. I eye the old television with bunny-ear antennae, then groan. My swollen belly is ready to burst. I go to the edge of the dirt-laden shack—the mansion, I mean—and sit at the window. A raven perches on the lone maple tree outside. "God!" it croaks. My eyes widen. "God!" it repeats. I press my face against the dust-caked window, then cough and wipe away the grime with my hand. "God!" it shrieks. I know the door is locked from the outside, but maybe the window?

I turn the lock, grasp at the frame, and pull. It doesn't budge. Of course. I try again. The wooden frame is old and begins to creak. I pull harder. It gives way as a pop reverberates through my body, and suddenly the floor at my feet is soaked. I lean on the window to shut it, but it won't return. Pain sears me and I collapse, writhing. Through the window, the raven cries, "God," mimicking me like an empathic midwife.

ooOOoo

Three days later, he returns. "Meet your sister," he says, thrusting a girl at least five years my junior at me. "She is my new helpmate, and she will help clean up the mess you've made." He eyes the small child, asleep at my feet on the blood-stained floorboards. "A girl," he says. And when I see the fire alight in his eyes, my converted heart turns to stone.

ooOOoo

Six months later, both of the helpmates of the mansion have swollen bellies. The difference is, her heart is converted, and mine is still stone. I don't tell him, though. When he enters the deepest caverns of my soul, I maintain Marian meekness. The fire in his eyes is a divine lamp seeking the truth, and he perceives in the deep blue wells of my eyes the subordinate heart that he—God—requires.

He does the same with her. Every single time, it's the same. As I suckle the baby, he plants his seed in the other helpmate, and she cries out. Her words are louder than mine, more piercing. She believes them, like I once did. She is fertile soil for God's planting.

She's starting to see behind my mask. She perceives not with fire but with icy blue water. She resents me for not believing. She hates me for lying to him. She avenges him by enjoying him with all the fervour of a true believer.

ooOOoo

Her baby is still-born, and he takes it from her. When he returns to the mansion, he orders her onto her knees to pray.

"Your soil was too rocky to be fruitful," he growled. "You shall not spill God's seed again. Your cup shall brim to the point of overflowing, and you shall not spill one drop. This is divine life being planted in you, handmaid. Now pray."

Her lifeblood flows onto the floor as he plants God's seed in her mouth, and I close my eyes, willing my bile back down. If I spill, I'll be next.

As he cries out, she blanches. "Don't you dare," he

4

snarls, and claps a hand over her mouth, pulling up his khakis with the other. She swallows her vomit, every drop, as her eyes burn hot with tears.

"I love you, Lord, my strength!" she cries, and his eyes soften. He kneels and draws her into a long embrace.

"All you need to do is listen to the Lord your God, and he will save you from eternal fire." She weeps as he strokes her hair. My heart grows black as tar.

oooOooo

I give birth again. Another girl. He's out saving souls again when it happens. He returns with a third helpmate, and this one barely has breasts.

"Now, you are my helpmates, and you are sisters, and you must learn to love one another for the sake of God," he says. "You will demonstrate your love for God by showing your love for one another. Do you understand?"

As the evening wears on, I think of the sign he carried with him on the day he met me. I wonder if the rules can bend whenever it suits God.

I decide that night that I no longer love the Lord my God, for he has made himself in the image of this man.

oooOooo

The next time he goes out, I wait an hour, then set to work. He didn't notice when I brought the woodaxe in the mansion after chopping up firewood that afternoon. I'm prepared to heave it at whatever stands between me and freedom.

The second helpmate sees me and howls as the axe falls on the door. She tries to wrench it from me, but I turn and kick her. She loses her wind. I turn back to the door and let the axe fall again, harder this time. She kicks my ankle and I collapse. She pulls my hair from behind me. I turn and bite her leg, piercing her flesh. She lets go of my hair and grabs her leg, hopping up and down like a kid on a pogo stick. Her pale straight hair and perky breasts jiggle, and as I stare at her, she grimaces and falls to the floor.

"You're naked," she spits. "You'll never make it out of here alive."

"You're naked," I answer in a low voice. "You'll never make it out of here alive."

I stand again, my head and ankle throbbing, and I destroy the rest of the door. The full moon is rising and the stars shine far more brightly than they ever have through the grimy windows. I pick up my daughters, nod at the third helpmate, and look once more at the second helpmate. She stares defiantly at me. With babies at my bare breasts, a naked girl at my side, and only the warmth of summer to cover my bare body, I walk out onto the wild landscape in freedom for the first time in twenty-one months.

ooOOoo

The television at the security guard's desk is on, and breaking news of a murder airs. I eat from the tree of knowledge now, and God doesn't notice.

"Police are investigating the gruesome discovery of a murder-suicide. Investigators say a teenage girl and thirty-five year old man were found dead at the site of a secluded, run-down cabin. Police Chief Adams reports that the girl slew the man with an axe before dismembering her hand with the same axe and bleeding to death. The identity of the two victims has not yet been discovered."

A bird chirps loudly in the background of the news report.

"God is dead," I mutter.

"What'd you say?" the security guard said, startled to see me there.

I eye the tree of knowledge for a moment before turning to go back to my sister, my daughters, and my unsoiled bed.

Kate is perpetually surprised by the worlds to which her writing transports her. She published her first anthology of short fiction and poetry, *Life. Love. Liturgy.*, in February 2014, and her work is published in several of Solarwyrm Press' publications. She's a thealogian (note: the "a" is no spelling error), the mom of two delightfully precocious girls, the spouse of an extraordinarily quirky man, and a baking temptress. Her writing is best known for its attention to marginalised and marginalising voices, and has been compared to the work of Flannery O'Connor. You can find her social networking links and read her blog, Thealogical Lady, at lifeloveliturgy.com

THE OUTCAST DEAD

BY GERALDINE CORNWALL

He gave me ten pounds and bought me a Knickerbocker Glory. I had never had so much money, not even on my birthday or Christmas or anything. And I had never had ice cream in a glass before. So many scoops and all for me. There was pink strawberry, chocolate flavour, butterscotch with crispy toffee bits all covered in golden nuts and loads of hundreds and thousands that looked like a kaleidoscope floating on the top. And it was smothered in chocolate and raspberry sauce that was flowing like a giant waterfall down the sides of the glass. I looked all around and nobody else had one. I felt really special. The ice cream looked so good that I almost couldn't bring myself to eat it. It started to melt, so Uncle John smiled and told me to eat it before it turned into a drink. I dipped the long spoon in and pulled out mouthful after mouthful. It was so good, I didn't want it to end. Uncle John was the best uncle in the whole world and he loved me more than anyone. All he wanted was to look at my front bottom. Five seconds, that's all it took. He looked so happy, smiled kindly at me and kissed me gently on the forehead. I loved him but I didn't know what he was looking at. Another part of me knew it was wrong so I told nobody.

Age 8, innocence taken.

It must have been almost a year when Uncle John came to stay again. We all went off to the beach in his Ford Corsair. He drove really fast. It was exciting. Jimmy and me started fighting in the back of the car. I caught Uncle John's eyes in the mirror. They were smiling at me. I felt special. I gave my brother one last hard punch in the face. His nose bled. I was happy. Uncle John stopped the car. He told me to sit in the front—passed a handkerchief to Jimmy to stem his bloody nose. He wiped the blood from my legs as he innocently pushed the polka dot dress up my thighs a little. The same time I felt his palm touch between the top of my legs. It tickled and felt nice—but I knew it was wrong. He smiled again and pushed the hair back from my face. We got to the beach. Jimmy and I jumped out of the car. I stayed close to him—I didn't want to be alone with Uncle John.

Age 9, childhood taken.

Uncle John visited regularly after that day. During the summers, he often drove us all to the beach for the day. Fifth of July 1967, we went to Blackpool for the day. I liked it there with the donkeys and the fairground rides. Screaming on the Wild Mouse as it hurtled to certain death along the weaving corkscrew of a rickety old track. He followed us down the beach carrying large cornets with whipped ice cream and two flakes in each. A red sauce that looked like blood flowed lavishly across the pale white waves of cream. It made me think of what some of the girls at school had been talking about—their periods. Mine still hadn't come. I wish it would come now, right now—this second, so that I wouldn't have to put my swimsuit on. I wanted my mum. Why didn't she come with us today? But no, she was getting a rest from us—getting her hair and nails done. Uncle John was so very good to mummy.

Age 11, virginity taken.

That was fourteen years ago. I finally told mum what was going on, on my sixteenth birthday. She didn't believe me. I had never seen her so wild—crazy. Her eyes like bullets that I thought would fire straight through me. I cowered in the corner—my nose pouring snot and blood from the mad slap she gave me.

Age 16, family taken.

That was the last time I was home. I ran and I ran and I ran. I have no recollection of stopping running, like it was only in that act that I remained alive. It killed the pain. Outcast, I awoke huddled in a dirty alley that smelt of men's urine. It was cold and dark. I was afraid. I lay there waiting for the day to come. It took forever. In that forever, I learned how to hate. I hated my uncle, I hated my mother, I hated God, I hated the world, but most of all I hated myself. It wasn't the first time in my life that I thought about killing somebody, although the clarity with which I conceived the executions this time was unprecedented. Can anyone honestly say that they have never thought about killing somebody?

Salvation came two days later in the unlikely guise of a beautiful, tall, blond knight with the most tender, watery, pale blue eyes that would soften the hardest heart. He found me in the park, my feet dangling below the swing seat. My arms locked around the left chain, my head tilted to the left hanging over my left shoulder. My wet, vacant eyes staring into a past that clung like a foul smell to a rabid dog. He sat on the swing next to mine. I didn't speak. He leaned into my swing and pulled the right chain his direction. My body was now facing him. The beautiful tender eyes crinkled very slightly as he smiled at me.

"Penny for them?" he asked, kindness in the eyes that never wavered from staring directly into mine.

It was the first human contact I had since I ran. I didn't answer. I felt the tears coming. I looked away and let the lank hair fall in front of my face to cover my shame.

He pulled again on the right chain repositioning me.

"You hungry?" he gently asked.

I nodded.

He smiled and put out his left hand. I put my pale white, right hand into it as I released myself from the left chain and stepped slowly to the ground. We walked to the café at the park entrance. He bought me a huge breakfast and two mugs of tea. I devoured it as he watched, all the time his eyes smiling tenderly. For two days he held me. He listened to me. He wiped away the tears that flowed like they would never end. He bathed me. He combed my hair. He clothed me in his soft, stripy flannelette pyjamas that were five sizes too big for me. For the first time I smiled.

When we finally made love it was like the earth swallowed us whole. We were so in love. When he touched me, I felt no guilt, I felt no shame. This was how it should be. God had delivered me. My life felt wonderful, blessed. I didn't even think about Mum, Uncle John, nothing. It all seemed so far away, another lifetime. Nothing could ruin my happiness. For the first time ever, I felt truly alive. I was free.

But sadly my knight turned out to be more pimp than prince. It was a typical Friday night get together. A few of Barry's mates would come over, bring a few beers and we'd all sit around laughing and telling jokes and stuff. They were a good crowd of guys and I enjoyed those nights.

This particular night, Barry was being really affectionate towards me, usually he held back in front of his mates, but this night he was giving me hugs, stroking my hair and occasionally kissing me lightly on the back of my head. It felt a little strange to be honest, but good, him making me feel so special in front of his friends. Anyway, it got to about 9.30 and one of the guys was quite drunk. He started telling us all how his girlfriend was pregnant, but it wasn't his. She had left him and moved in with the father of the unborn baby. He was in a right state, crying and all that. Barry went over to him, put his arm around his shoulder and gave him another beer. I couldn't hear what Barry said to him, but after a few moments he stopped crying and pulled himself together. Barry came back over to me on the settee and popped his right arm around my shoulder pulling me closer to him and whispered how he loved me. I squeezed his right thigh with my left hand and leaned my head into his chest. I felt safe, happy and proud. Next thing, Barry squeezes me a little harder pulling me even closer to him and whispers

"He's in a bad way honey, he needs some loving—give him some—please honey—do it—do it for me."

I sat up rigid, unsure of what I had heard. I turned and looked at him thinking it was a sour joke. His eyes told me immediately that it wasn't. He was totally serious.

"Please—for me." His words poisoned arrows that pierced my soul.

But I loved him, so I agreed. He was pleased. All the time his mate was fucking me, Barry stood by the door, watching. I was numb. I made not one noise. I looked at Barry the whole time, staring into his eyes, pleading with mine for his help. He looked straight back at me, his eyes cold steel blue. When he had finished, he climbed off me. As he went through the door I saw him give Barry something. To this day I have no idea what I was worth that night.

After that, Barry wouldn't even look at me, let

alone talk to me. He would punch me for kicks. He would smash my face into the mirror if something upset him. I had no idea what had happened.

Age 17, trust taken.

The beatings and sex became more violent and more frequent. He kept me upstairs, locked in a grubby, dark room at the back of the house. There was a small skylight window that didn't open. When I stood on a chair, I could see across the tops of the grey slate roofs into an endless nothingness. I saw rain and smog. I never knew when the next trick would be delivered nor what degradation demanded. My body was a grey tapestry of scars that bore witness to the floggings and abuses. Some of the whips had nails tied into them that would tear into my flesh with each lash. I came to enjoy the pain that inflicted, as its intensity allowed me to escape briefly the despair of my reality. Others used knives and broken bottles to leave their mark on my body. All manner of objects thrust into my dead vagina to bring sordid satisfaction to these pitiable excuses for humanity. Not one tear did I shed. At each encounter, I mumbled a penance of Hail Mary's—begging the Holy Virgin to plead for me with the ever absent God. The repetition slighted the blows.

The crippled mare was now totally broken. Nothing mattered anymore. Yet in a strange way, this absolute brokenness gave me a sense of power. There was nothing that anyone could do to me anymore that could hurt me, that could damage me, that could touch me.

Age 20, hope taken.

I recall a sermon I once heard a young South American priest give at St Mildred's about forgiveness. How it is in that act we find freedom and redemption. It meant little to me then and even less to me now. I feel no forgiveness in my heart and nor do I want to. I feel bitterness. I feel anger. I feel hatred. Hatred to the world, to myself and to the God that long ago abandoned me, if he were ever there at all. I was born into chains, kept in chains and punished in chains. I never had choices. And all of this overseen by the all loving, omnipotent, omniscient God. I will leave forgiveness for Him. And I wonder who forgives Him. To ask it from me would be the biggest degradation of all.

Age 21, faith taken.

And so now, in my final act of defiance, self-empowerment and control, I seize my own freedom. I walk to the dingy corner of the room, stepping behind the dirty torn curtain to the area that serves as a toilet. It stinks of men's urine. I open the cracked mirrored door of the battered cabinet. I pick up the blade with my right hand. I carefully and quietly close the cabinet door with my left hand. For a brief moment I see my reflection in the cracked mirror. I look away. I don't think. I turn my focus to the blade in my right hand. I hold it firm and upright between my forefinger and thumb. With absolute precision, unwavering certainty and commitment, I cut deeply across the blue veins protruding high from the wrist of my outstretched left arm. I stand still, unmoved. I watch waves of the most precious blood of Our Lady, The Holy Virgin Mother of God, flow lavishly across the creamy white flesh. For the first time I smile in victory, as I offer myself up willingly and eternally into the welcoming and warm embrace of the Outcast Dead.

Geraldine Cornwall is British, currently living in London. In addition to writing, she also paints, using an abstract impressionist style, frequently creating artworks that leave the viewer to fill in the gaps, and she finds herself employing a similar technique in her writing. She has recently started to combine her writing and painting in illustration.

She often finds stimulus for her work, both directly and indirectly, from travels. She has travelled much in Asia, Africa, South and Central America, The Middle East and India. She likes to be spontaneous in her approach, reacting to an event or events and then delivering that response.

If in any way, no matter how small, she can use her writing and/or painting to help give voice to those who struggle to be heard, she feels privileged to be able to do so. The plight of the school girls taken hostage in Nigeria was extremely distressing and she felt compelled to respond. She has for some time been a supporter of the A21 Campaign, which offers support to victims of human trafficking and works with law enforcement agencies to bring the perpetrators to court. You can see her work at: http://thiswomanswork2014.tumblr.com/writer

THE RISING

BY JAX GOSS

She rises.

For too long her head has been bowed and her voice has been soft. For years, it seems, lifetimes even, she has stood silent and quiet, head bent and arms demurely at her sides, taking what they dish out, flinching at the blows and guarding her heart against the lies and the slights and the insults they fling at her. She has held her freedom out and let them chain her. She has quashed her own spirit singing for flight, and she has lowered her eyes and demurred.

But today she rises.

When she came here she fought like a wild thing, with all the fire and outrage of a youth enchained. She spat in their faces, and looked them in the eyes, her mouth turned in a sneer, her heart adamant that she could not be tamed, could not be broken. She was wrong.

They broke her. They beat her body and they twisted her soul into bitter blackness, until it became easier to lower her eyes and her voice, to wrap herself in silence, to hope for rescue. And finally to give up all hope. To resign herself to a lifetime lived in servitude, in shuffling silent slavery. Hardly a lifetime at all, simply a passing of time until death. Do what must be done to survive. Be silent. Be invisible.

But today she rises.

It is not a special day. It is a day like any other, with a hot sun rising over a dry world, and the taunting sounds of birdsong. She wakes, and raises her eyes to the sun, and she knows that today she will not be silent any more. Today she will be visible, today she will lift her eyes, and if they hurt her for it, then they do.

She stands up in the world, surrounded by her sisters all still trying to sleep, grabbing the last moments of rest they can, and she looks out at the rising sun, and she thinks, *Today, me too. Today I rise with you, sister sunlight.*

They line up as always, and the man walks down the line, his hard eyes gliding across a series of downcast and beaten faces. When he reaches her, he stops. Her eyes are bright, her face uplifted. He stops before her, and stares into her face. She says nothing, yet, but she looks back, eyes hard and bright and level.

"You," he says. "What is your number?"

She looks right at him and says, "I am not a number. My name is Rana."

The blow when it comes is ringing and violent, and she falls to the ground, the taste of blood in her mouth. He is moving away, when she struggles, standing back to her feet.

She rises. Eyes proud, face uplifted.

He turns. He comes back. His voice is low, menacing and predatory.

"Your number, slave?"

"Rana," she says.

This time the blow hits her in her stomach, and she

falls to her knees. Getting up is harder now, and he is further away by the time she does, but she smiles through the taste of blood, and in a soft, strong voice says, "Rana."

He stops walking and turns back to her. He moves close, using the size of his body, trying to shrink her, intimidate her. "You are nobody. You are nothing. You are a number."

She looks into his eyes, dark with hatred, and says, "I am Rana."

This time when he hits her she blacks out.

When she wakes, one of the other girls is sponging her forehead, where he has burst her head open, her blood flowing. "That wasn't smart. You know there's no fighting back."

"Maybe not," says Rana. "But what if we all did it? What if all we did was reclaim our names? No one is coming, and the other option is to live as grey numbers forever. What if we rise?"

The other girl clicks her tongue in frustration and reproach.

But the next day, when Rana once again tells the man her name, four other girls do it too.

I am Rana. I am Haske. I am Fata. I am Mai. I am Ganguna.

They are all beaten.

The next day it is twelve. A week later fifty. The next week all of them.

Today they rise. Today they have names.

Jax Goss is an editor and writer. She is also a wandering South African who seems to have settled in New Zealand. She lives in Dunedin, for the moment. She is currently employed full time as the mother of a very small human, and writes and edits on the side. She expects this situation to stay the same for a while, but she has long ago learnt that nothing ever goes the way she expects.

She spends a large amount of her time gathering tales and poems and art and sending them out into the world in various forms, and thinks that this may be her vocation. You can follow her wayward journey at her website: jaxgoss.wordpress.com.

SLAVE: THE STORY OF ALINA X

BY DEBBIE LECHTMAN

This mirror reminds me of my mama, which is just so strange because I know nothing about her. Nothing. The edges are decorated with fine golden swirls, nice and classy. Expensive, certainly. Perhaps an antique. Looks Turkish to me.

The glass is clear, shiny. No rust. No questionable stains. Bam! My reflection hits me right in the gut. I pucker my pink little lips like a heart, smooth my thick bangs over my forehead so the strands don't stick out all funny like they do. I make sure to cover my left eye.

I can't show that to anyone.

"Are you ready, Alina?" someone says from outside the dressing room. I don't recognise the voice, but it's a woman; it could be the intern—Ronit, Sarit?—or maybe Liora, the producer.

I keep staring at my reflection in the mirror and think about how pretty and how ugly I look.

A knock. "Alina?"

I snap out of it, trace the lines of my mouth with bright red lipstick. Whore lipstick. Ha-ha. "One second," I try to say, but the words get caught somewhere high up in my throat. "Just a minute."

I won't ever be ready for this.

Another knock, then two more. My face feels hot all of a sudden, like I've done something wrong. I haven't, though. "One minute," I say finally, my words hoarse like my breath.

My breath is always thick like syrup.

"OK. Whenever you're ready, Alina."

"Sure."

"We're waiting for you."

"I know. I'm coming."

I spin around on my spidery legs, away from the mirror and into the world.

oooOooo

The truth is that I never knew Mama. I got stuffed into the stinky, overcrowded Russian orphanage at six months and I never saw her again. No one ever told me why she got rid of me—it's not like the Russian government to divulge information like that, especially not then, memories of the Soviet Union still painful and fresh—and the only thing that ties me back to her is my name. Alina. Alina X. Everything else, they took away.

Sometimes I wonder whether she was a prostitute like me, whether my papa was her pimp or maybe her client, a respectable doctor or lawyer with a secret life on the side. I wonder whether this badness was inside my bones before I could do anything to stop it. I like to think so, anyway. I don't feel so guilty that way. You see, it's not *me,* Officer, sir; it's genetics. And there is nothing you can do to stop genetics.

It is what it is.

I liked the Russian orphanage at first. We played games when the nuns weren't looking and got three square meals a day, also. When I was a baby, I didn't even have any real duties, no cleaning or making the beds or anything. All I had to do was sit there and gargle, blubber, drool. The older girls were like mamas to me—I remember Nastya and Tanya and Anya—they kissed me on the forehead and on the lips sometimes, and I would get a whiff of their knockoff *amerikansy* perfume, or I'd feel their chunky blue mascara against my skin. They said it would all be fine and that they'd protect me, and of course I believed them, because I was a child and children will eat just about anything right up. When I grew a little older I was supposed to go to school, but I almost always skipped lessons to hang out with the big girls in the alleys. Sometimes they were really kind to me and offered me a puff or two of their cigarettes, but the smoke burnt my throat. I remember how my eyes watered; I wheezed and sputtered until I thought maybe I'd accidentally coughed my lungs out. But the girls, Nastya and Tanya and Anya, they looked so sophisticated, their long, pointy red nails flicking the ash to the ground.

I was happy.

ooOOoo

"You don't have to answer any of the questions. If you feel uncomfortable, I mean."

"Of course."

"Seriously, though. I mean it." The wiry intern, the one with springy red hair and horse teeth—whose name, it turns out, is neither Sarit nor Ronit but actually Tal—squeezes my hand really tight. I wish she'd get off me. I don't like it when they touch me.

But I smile, and I feel the left side of my face caving in, where there's the hole I can't talk about to anyone, ever. "It's all right, really," I say. "I want to do this. Really. It'll be... what is it you Tel Aviv University people say?" I try to say it is a joke, but it doesn't come out that way.

"Cathartic?"

"Yes. Cathartic. Yeah. It'll be cathartic for me."

"All right, everybody ready?" the director yells from his high black chair in his black jeans and black t-shirt. And black, thick-rimmed glasses. *So hipster*, I think. It's the new fashion among the Tel Aviv twenty and thirty-somethings, this stupid hipster thing. He's so short his legs dangle stupidly from his hips, and if he didn't have such a thick gray beard, I'd think he was a small child or something.

The cameraman gives him the thumbs up, but his eye is glued to the peephole.

"Awesome," the director says offhandedly, and I feel a mass growing and growing like a herpes sore inside my throat. "Cool." The lights are so bright and yellow and hot, and I wish I could take my clothes off and run away screaming. I'm not ready. I'm just not. No one cares, though, that I'm not ready. No one ever cares about me—that's for sure.

"All right, then... lights... camera... action!"

Somebody claps the marker—snap!—and now I feel the bile rising from my stomach to my throat to my mouth. It takes everything I have not to vomit all over myself. The snap startled me.

"So," some woman says, and it takes me a few seconds to realise she's right here next to me, in her fancy, European-style, well-pressed black suit and her powdery face makeup. "Let's begin. Could you tell me your name?"

I swallow the bad taste in my mouth. "Alina," I say, and my voice is so frail no one would ever guess I speak three languages and read in four.

She blinks; her big, fake eyelashes flutter. I feel an urge to steal them, rip them right off her skin. See the droplets of inky blood trickling out. "Alina? Alina what?" she says, her smile to her ears and her teeth white like fresh snow, like the snow we'd see back in Russia sometimes if we were far enough from the city gray.

"Alina what?" I repeat, and I feel increasingly dumb. Alina what?

The corners of her hazel eyes tense a little. I can tell she thinks I'm the most foolish girl she's ever interviewed. "Last name," she says, still pleasant. I want to pull out her perfect eyelashes so bad. "What's your last name?"

"I don't have a last name," I say with a shrug.

Alina X.

She giggles, really high-pitched and awkward, and I can sense her discomfort. There is a strain in the room; the air feels thick and sticky. "You don't know your last name, Alina?" I can tell she thinks perhaps I'm joking, like I'm playing a game on her.

I'm not.

Alina X.

"It's not that I don't know it," I say, and I'm trying really hard to keep my voice even. Something in me wants to snap. The left side of my face twitches, an uncontrollable convulsion. "I don't have one."

She wants to be anywhere but here, in this chilly, over-illuminated studio, I can see that. I do, too. "You—you don't have a last name? How can you not have a last name?"

"Huh," I say, and I smile a little bit. "Don't know." Right away, I know to cover my mouth with my hand because five of my teeth are missing, and the last thing that I want is to be on a Channel 2 documentary looking like *another* Russian whore.

That's all we are to them. To the Jews. To the Arabs.

"Do you—um, do you know what it was at birth? You're originally from Russia, aren't you?" she asks, her yellow-lined eyes big and round, hopeful. They look like finely carved wood. She's stumbling, stuttering.

She's very pretty though.

I shrug my shoulders and shake my head softly from side to side. "Nope."

Now I can make out a trickle of sweat beads on her forehead. I wonder if she's getting nervous that I'm ruining her interview. That's how it is here in Israel—everybody fears a scandal, because chances are you'll be next. "Would anyone know it?"

I shrug again. "Maybe the first orphanage I was at," I say. I want to help her. I really do. "In Russia. But I don't remember what that place was called. And it might not even exist anymore."

She flicks her wrist to the side and laughs shrilly, like she already knows this interview's down the drain and I've fucked it up for everyone and God help me, I can't do anything right. I half expect her to start crying on the spot, like her career is over because of my stupidity or something, but instead she gathers herself quickly and says, "Maybe we'll come back to that later, then."

My cheeks get hot. What kind of fool doesn't know her own last name? But I say, "Okay."

She perks right up, straightens her back a little against the chair. "Can you tell me anything about your home life? Your family? Your parents?"

"Um," I say, growing damp and flustered. My throat starts closing and I just want to get out at all costs. But my butt is glued to the chair, like I've got no other choice. "Um, well. I was taken into the orphanage when I was really little. Six months."

She makes a little *o* shape with her lips, like that's the saddest thing she's ever heard. "Wow," she says. "That's rough. Do you know anything about them?"

"Um. Not really. I used to imagine what they were like, though."

"What would you imagine?"

Shit. I said too much. "Um, I don't know, really. Mostly my mother. I thought maybe she had problems like me, and that's why she gave me up. And it made me feel better thinking, you know, that my problems were genetic. Like I couldn't do anything to fix them or stop them, so it wasn't my fault after all."

She furrows her brows. The light brown freckles on her forehead ripple like tiny waves. "Problems like you?" What do you mean by that? Do you mean—"

"Yeah, that she was a whore like me, yeah. A prostitute."

"Is that what you see yourself as?" she whispers, and now I realise she's forgotten she's interviewing me at all.

I shrug. "Sure."

Her eyes are sad now. I can see sadness in eyes like some people can predict pregnancies or deaths or whatever. It's my gift. I can even see the sadness in my own eyes. Eye, rather. "But Alina," she says. "You're only fourteen."

Debbie Lechtman is a 23-year-old fiction writer and editor currently living in Austin, TX. She grew up in both Israel and Costa Rica but prefers writing in English, even though it is technically her third language. Besides reading and writing, Debbie enjoys travelling, making jewelry (she runs a small jewelry store on Etsy called TheRockShopAustin), bike riding and hiking, and spending time with her two-year-old mutt, Simba. You can learn more about Debbie and her work by visiting debbielechtman.com.

MOONLIT MEMORIES

BY ALANA GARRIGUES

"Everyone is a moon, and has a dark side which he never shows to anybody." —Mark Twain

Naka

Togo

One month after my Mamma started her monthly bleeding, my Granddaddy sold her for fifteen dollars.

She ain't mad at him. Granddaddy and Grandmamma had lots of mouths to feed, she tells me. They didn't want to get rid of her. They just couldn't afford to keep her.

"Them babies needed food," she says. "Granddaddy sacrificed your Mamma to feed those babies. He had to, baby girl. But he loved your Mamma. He had a smile and laugh that rocked this earth, baby. It hurt him something fierce, giving me away—I ain't never seen another man cry like the day he gave me away. Grandmamma just looked away and went in to tend to the others, but I know she was hurtin' too."

Mamma is a good Mamma.

She don't talk much about the man my Granddaddy sold her to. Except to say he was a mean old coot. Thirty-some-odd years her senior, always shouting at her in Ewe. Mamma don't speak Ewe. She grew up speakin' Kabye, so she didn't know what he was saying. Just that he was mad as the devil.

At first, Mamma'd do her best, she said. But he didn't like her. Didn't like no woman, I suppose, 'cause I don't see how someone can't like my Mamma.

She'd show up at the well to gather water, eyes black, with a broken lip, and the other women shunned her.

Shakin' they heads, and whisperin' things like, "That girl is trouble. Why she don't just submit to her man? Make it easier on herself. Don't she know her place?"

My Mamma hated them women, as much as she admired them. They looked tired and swollen and sometimes beat too, but they had each other.

They didn't know my Mamma tried to submit. Now she say she didn't know they mostly shamed her because they were afraid their husbands would see them showing her pity, get afraid they'd be difficult too. Men are often afraid, she says, of the power of women talkin' too much.

She took it for a while, went about her business, gatherin' water and cookin' and cleanin' 'til her hands cramped up.

But then my Mamma got mad. That Mamma of mine, she got spunk.

She went to that man's Pastor and confessed her sins—and his. The Pastor took it out on that man my Granddaddy sold my Mamma to, telling him he weren't welcome at church until he sorted out his wife. Took away his Sunday rights, made a spectacle of him.

That man, he took it out on my Mamma. Stopped givin' her food. Made sure whatever she cooked, he ate it all up. She lost weight, stopped her monthly bleeding.

She told me she got so hungry, she started picking for bugs off the floor for protein, licking water thrown out with the neighbour's cooking. But then, one day, she got mad again, decided a lonely life wasn't no life at all. Said she missed singin' and dancin' and livin'.

So she started to fight back. Kickin' and shoutin' and pullin' on his hair. Even bitin' when he came close enough. Took a chunk out of his thumb, she told me once.

He got fed up—called my Granddaddy and tried to sell her back.

Granddaddy said no way—another baby, and still no work. He couldn't afford to take my Mamma back.

So, that's how she came to my Daddy.

My Daddy'd been widowed. His wife died in childbirth, taking herself and their twins. He needed somebody to tend to his home, and he needed somebody cheap because he'd just spent all his money on the funerals.

Daddy bought my Mamma from that man. Real cheap, on account of all the trouble she'd put 'im through. My Daddy told her when he bought her that he'd take good care of her, that she'd never want for nothin', as long as she did what a wife needed to do. Soon as she was healed, body and soul, she'd have to keep the house just right. But, he warned, if she tried to run off or bed some other man, Lord help her.

For three months, my Mamma says he fed her, let her rest, got her nice and plumped up again. Introduced her to the neighbours and took her to church with 'im. Then, he told her it was time she started her womanly duties—makin' babies and cookin' and cleanin' all on her own. And that's how I came to be. First baby, screamin' loud as a goat in labour when I was born, my Mamma tells me. She was just fifteen, but she says I was the best thing that ever happened to her.

Daddy says I was his first real love—he's happy with Mamma, and has grown to love her, but she's still his.

He still don't know if she stays because she loves him or because he told her she had to all those years back. He stood by his promise. She works to please, and he treats her good. I think she loves him, but she don't talk about it any.

Daddy says he never knew a full heart 'til he had me. Says he'd never sell me like my Granddaddy sold my Mamma, no matter.

I sure do hope it's true. Cause my lady bleeding started up last night, right with the full moon. I told my Mamma 'bout the red between my thighs, and she just held me tight. Rockin' me back and forth, like a baby, singin' the songs her Mamma and Daddy sang when the moon went down. Back when she was small.

ooOOoo

Arjana
Rome
As the sun sets and the moon rises, thousands of candles start to flicker. Voices of those holding the votives begin to hum, filling Vatican Square with a chilling serenity.

I shouldn't be here. I should be across town, walking my street, racking up my sins that most of the residents of the Vatican might say will prevent me from ever entering the pearly gates.

I don't believe them. I know I've still got good in my heart, and I think the Holy Father knows that too. He sees what I've done, but He knows it's not all my choice. Just like His son loved Mary Magdalene.

Mary Magdalene is our saving grace. All us streetwalkers know that if Jesus loved her and trusted her, we were gonna be okay in the end.

But still, I try to avoid the Vatican and all the churches across town. They usually frown on "unsavoury" characters like me standing outside. Plus, we don't earn so much there. Something about a church makes a man think twice before opening his wallet for a blowjob.

And yet, I'm here, standing in Vatican Square because there's no place else I could be right now. I know I'll be lucky to make it through the night, once they find me, but it's the price I have to pay.

Luljeta, or Luli, as I called her, was a friend. She was younger than me, so I sort of took her under my wing. I have to honour her memory.

We fell into this business in much the same way. "Foreigners" born in a xenophobic land. Especially against our people—Albanians. We were ridiculed, blamed for everything wrong—unemployment, high cost of government programs, violence, robbery, the demise of the family structure. It was all our fault. Us and the Algerians. Something about Al nationalities... They don't want to understand us, or they want to think they're somehow different, that by distancing from us, they won't catch civil unrest or poverty. I don't know.

Anyway, when Luli was about 14, she met a man. He was older, 25, she thinks. Handsome, funny, a big risk taker. Paid attention to her, and made life fun. Made her believe, for the first time in her life, that she could be a part of something, instead of the one cast aside. One afternoon, after a midday rendezvous in the bedroom, he offered her a cig. She didn't know it at the time, but it was laced with coke.

She loved how it felt, so he gave her more. And more. Eventually, he couldn't afford her habit, so she started to reach out, expand her possibilities. A hand job here, some light sadomasochism there, always in exchange for some dope.

That's the problem with drugs. They make you do things you wouldn't usually do, just craving that high. Eventually, she crossed the wrong guys. They kept her high as a kite, took turns on her, passed her around like some kind of rental car or something. Put her up in an apartment.

Her parents tried to go to the police, but—no proof of a crime, no proof that she was Italian, they ignored it. Told them she must've runaway. She'd be back.

But girls like that, they don't come back. Girls like me.

By the time she was 16, she was working the streets, trying to pay off the "rent" and food and drugs they kept her with. She didn't keep her earnings, of course, but as long as she was high, she didn't seem to mind too much. Didn't realise her situation.

That's when I met her. We were working a couple of streets apart, had some of the same handlers in common from over the years. I started to talk to her when we could, share a cigarette, chat about our childhoods, the men who made us believe they loved us, the drugs that felt so good, so numbing, so right.

It's not like we liked life roaming the streets. But we had no choice, and it satisfied at least some of our needs. We figured things could be worse. We could actually be living on the streets, instead of our dingy, crowded apartments. At least this way, we get our fix.

Then one day, something changed in her. I saw it in her eyes. I think she saw someone, someone she knew from long ago. A cousin, or an old friend, maybe. It happens sometimes. I don't know. But a light switched on in her head, and all in a flash, it was like she understood.

That's the thing about girls like me. Once we realise, it's too late. We accept that it must be this way, and that's it. We fuck strangers, we give all our money to men who watch us, every second of every day, and they feed us drugs.

It's not the life a little girl dreams of, but it's a life.

Thing about Luli is, once she actually realised it, once she saw that ghost from her past, she figured out that she wasn't one of us. Couldn't accept that she ever was. Said she was going to sober up, get back to school, see her family. Maybe help other kids steer clear of her mistakes, get into local politics.

Big dreams for a woman with no future. I didn't know she'd actually try.

One night, she walked right into the police station.

Bold move—paid a guy who picked her up to take her there instead of whatever he'd planned. Said she saw the car seat in the back of the car and the ring on his finger, started talking about how God saw everything and hadn't he promised to honour his wife. Something like that. Guilted him into it.

But the police wouldn't do a thing. Told her they didn't deal with runaways, didn't want things to get messy. So they turned her out.

She had no choice. Went back to her handler. Got beat pretty bad. Didn't show up on the corner for a couple of weeks.

And when she did, she stepped right in front of the first police car that passed. I suppose she thought they'd have to pay attention then. I don't think she meant for what happened next. Maybe she did.

The officer couldn't stop. It was too late, too quick. She was dead on impact.

At 17, the new face of forced prostitution, the new warning signal to empower young girls, believe in them, and tell them to believe in themselves. The new call to the police to pay attention to girls on the streets.

So now I stand here, miles from my post and my pimp, amongst thousands of mourners. But I know the truth. I know yesterday, they would have walked right past her, paying no attention. Maybe a few would have stopped and offered her cash for a favour. The rest would have averted their eyes, paid no attention to a hooker on the corner.

I am the only one who really knew her. I am the one who deserves this moment.

And I wonder—would she be happier that thousands were gathered in her name, finally aware, or that she had one true friend, standing here, risking it all, to remember?

oooOooo

Svetlana

Washington, DC

Stupid fucking American dream. Bullshit promise of a "better life," capitalism, feminist power. Fuck that.

"Go to America," my Aunt Viktoriya said. "Go find yourself a man who wants to make something of himself. Get an education. Get married. Make some money. Have lots of fucking babies. I don't care. But leave Russia. The Cold War may be over, but the old boy KGB network will never die. Go to America."

"Shut up," my father said. "Svetlana is Russian. She belongs in Russia, with her family."

"Don't forget—she also has some gypsy blood in her. I left my family for you," said my mother. "Let her go. Let her get a little sun, a little 'culture'. She'll come back, when she's ready."

So we surfed the net, found a website promising work and Visas for girls with the right talents—limited English speakers, attractive, with attention to customer service. The pay was high for Russia, low for America, but promised free room and board. I applied, sent in a picture, and got a hit in minutes. Jobs available in the American capital.

A photo of a man with kind eyes spoke to me, and I applied to stay with him during my homestay. Young, successful, a little rugged, with an interest in Russian culture. His name was Jed. Within weeks, I had my plane ticket.

My grandfather dropped me off at the airport.

A tear in his eye, he pulled me in and said, "Don't trust those fucking American pieces of shit. Your mother, your father, they believe the Cold War is over. It ain't. Listen to what I say. Don't fucking trust an American. They will pillage a Russian any chance they get. Come back soon."

I love that wrinkled, loving, ignorant old man of a grandfather, I thought to myself. *I'm gonna miss him, old school fucking commie paranoia and all.*

Next day, I touched down in Dulles, cleared customs

and security, and found an old guy with a fucking unlit cigar and a potbelly holding a sign with my name. Must be the chauffeur, I figured.

I should have run. I should have told Immigration I was here to work, instead of "on vacation" like the agency instructed me. I should have shoved my black leather stiletto right into his fucking balls, right then and there. But I trusted the photo of good old blue eyes and got in the old guy's car.

ooOOoo

One. Two. Three. Four. Five. Six locks slide open.

I hear the key shoved into the door. I hear it turn, one, two, three times, unlocking the barrier that keeps me here. How long have I been here? Days? Weeks? Months? Years? I quit counting a long fucking time ago.

Pot Belly isn't dead, and with how much booze he drinks and hard knocks he takes, it can't have been too long. Maybe two years, probably three. My mind is playing tricks on me. That's what captivity does. Seconds draw out like years, and months run together like days. I don't fucking know anymore. I wonder if my parents know. I wonder if my parents are still alive. I wonder if they look for me, desperate to find out why their daughter went quiet, or whether they think I landed here and betrayed their memory, set to 80 hour work weeks and building my own life. That's what people used to do. Write a letter now and then, but try to dull the pain of loss through neglect.

Sometimes I write to them in my mind and press send, or imagine neatly folded stationary which I postmark, air mail. Sometimes I write about my truth. Sometimes I tell a string of lies—I joined the circus and travel from city to city, a star gymnast drowning in Swarovski crystals, a source of Russian pride for all the ex-pats I meet along the way.

The door opens and I struggle to make it to a corner.

Fetal position works best. When he's really fucking wasted, he can't untangle my limbs. A few swift kicks to the ribs and elbow jabs to the head, and he gives up, leaves me be.

But the less I eat, the less strength I have to stay curled up.

oooOooo

We pulled into the driveway—manicured lawns, shuttered windows. Anxious to meet Jed, hoping the homestay would lead to more of a carnal affection, I hop out of the car. Pot Belly insists on being a gentleman and carries my bag into the hallway.

I walk through the front door and—BAM—knocked out with something heavy and cold to the back of my head.

I wake up groggy, confused.

Pot Belly sits in front of me.

"Where's Jed?" I ask.

"You're fuckin' lookin' at him, you stupid fuckin' cunt."

"Hey, eff you," I growl through my pain and thick accent. "That can't be right. His eyes are blue; yours are brown. Where did you take me? Where's my bag? I need to find Jed, and I need to report to the agency that I've arrived and I'm ready to work tomorrow."

"I took you exactly where you belong, bitch. You're mine now. I am your fucking job now. There's no agency, no blue eyes. That photo was some damn underwear model all the chicks dig. Bait, I think you'd call it. And your precious bag? Burned. Phone, photos, passport, gone. You're fucking nobody. Don't try to run, doll, because nobody here gives a shit about an ex Russian mail order piece of ass. This is DC, baby. Land of screwed up politicians and diplomats with immunity. People here tend to disappear, so don't. Fucking. Try. They won't believe you."

Mail order? I have no idea what he is talking about.

But that doesn't matter. I need to know who this man is.

"Who are you?"

"I am your master, and your destiny. That's all you need to know."

This time, I black out on my own.

ooOOoo

The door creaks open. I can hear his boots shuffle in the dark. Why he insists on wearing them, I will never know. Maybe that's why he never found a normal relationship. Who wants to fuck a man who wears boots to bed?

I try to hide, but I know it's futile. I know he'll find me. The dark only protects a woman alone in a small room for so long.

ooOOoo

When I come to that first day, I'm naked, strapped to a bed. Pot Belly is tearing into me. I've never been so angry or so humiliated. The shutters are closed, but I see a sliver of moonlight, and I think of my mother.

"When you see the moon, blow me a kiss. I'll catch it on the other side."

I pucker up and pray she gets it, a tear rolling down my cheek.

ooOOoo

"Svetlana," he slurs. "I'm comin' ta get ya. Where you at? Big Poppa's had a bad day, and it's time for a little fun."

I don't know what he does. I don't know if his name is Jed. Sometimes I do hear the front door open and close, so I think he goes somewhere. But, for all I know, he might not work. He might have murdered the family that used to live in this house and stolen their

39

identities. He might be a United States Lobbyist. He might be a Professor. He might be a goddamn garbage man. I don't know. All I know is no one has ever come to the house. No one but me. At least as long as I've been here. Maybe there was another woman before me.

What I do know, is that slurring and "bad days" mean real fucking pain for me.

After that first day, he let me out of my room sometimes during the day. Mostly to clean the house and order me around, but I could cook and clean. I cherished the chores I had hated at home, because they made me feel normal, human. I couldn't leave the house, or walk near a window, or go within six metres of a computer, but I could move and stay active.

Being stuck in a room most of the day makes you start to doubt your humanity, your worth. Makes you wonder what other ugly you've lived around your whole life. Then you give up, and embrace your animal instincts. Fear, anger, competition. Thoughts hurt too much.

Every night, I was locked back up, behind permanently shuttered windows, gagged to silence me, and prodded in every orifice.

Then, one day, I tried to make my escape. I thought he was gone, and I started banging on the walls, screaming, jumping on the bed, hoping to make enough sound to alarm a neighbour, a dog, anyone. Only one person heard. "Jed."

He stormed into my room, boots on, a belt in each hand, and beat me within an inch of my life. My blood pooling on the floor and the walls, he left me limp. Came back a minute later with a bottle of vodka. My vodka. The thank you gift from my Aunt for blue eyed Jed, my handsome host on this American journey, to express her appreciation for sharing his home and his culture with her dear Svetlana. Apparently, Pot Belly had pulled that out of my luggage before the fire to burn the rest of my belongings.

"Cheers," he boasted, before pouring it on my sliced

wounds. "The alcohol will sterilise your cuts. Should keep you alive. You're welcome, by the way."

Then he raped me again, stopping every so often to lick the mixture of vodka and blood from my skin.

I haven't been let out of my room since.

ooOOoo

He's found me. Tonight, he doesn't bother with untangling my limbs. He goes straight for the hair and drags me across the floor to my mattress in the middle of the room, knocking over my pot of rancid ochre pee along the way, mumbling, "shit," as he does.

I only wish it were, I think.

As he ties my hands and feet, I glimpse out of the centimetre of space between the shutters and the top board of the window, and for a moment, I catch a sliver of the moon. I blow a silent kiss, and remember my mother, feeling human again.

ooOOoo

Khalid
Dubai
Chink. Chink. Chink.

I sit beside my bed, waiting for my turn to sleep, and toss rocks on the cement floor.

Chink. Chink. Chink.

The three men in my bed don't stir. Manual labour does that to a man. Sixteen hours, every day, high atop the skyline of Dubai. We start before the sun comes up, and finish after the mosquitoes have gone to sleep. Banging and hammering and welding the skyscrapers of the future.

Then we come home, and take turns sleeping four hours a piece. Six men to a bed. Three for the first shift, three for the second. Four beds to a room. Twenty-four men living together in a beat up trailer, thrown together by destiny.

Chink. Chink. Chink.

I'm the only one tossing pebbles. The man next to me fell asleep sitting upright. He snores, occasionally batting his hand at a fly that lands on his nose. Another uses a stick to write imaginary notes to the wife and child he left behind, promising to send money and build a better life for all of them. Beyond him, one plays Ludo alone, muttering, "Get out of a prison, please, Allah, send me a six."

Growing up in Pakistan, I looked to the United Arab Emirates as the place where Muslim dreams come true. Wealth and western stores combined with a nod to Islamic culture. It seemed like they had it all figured out compared to my own country, where families struggle to put food on the table, and monsters terrorise their fellow man in the name of Allah. Allah couldn't be on their side, I knew. I wasn't sure he was on the side of Dubai wealth either, but at least I thought he would prefer their civility.

When a job opportunity appeared in the paper, giving Pakistani men the chance to live in Dubai and gain skills in constructing the world's tallest buildings, all expenses covered, I jumped. I could worship Allah and build a future for myself and my family. I would go, and send money home to my parents and sisters and brothers, learn about progressive cultures, and return with a vision for a better Pakistan.

So I went.

My first day, the HR manager brought me in. He told me he'd need my passport to get all my paperwork in order. He'd give it back soon, he promised. I handed it over. That was eight years ago. I never saw it again.

"Oh, the government must've lost it processing your Visa," he said. "Don't worry, you'll get another."

Except another never comes. Not for me. Not for any of the twenty-four men in my trailer. New HR men come all the time, but none of them seem to find our passports. Not for any of the thousands of men I work beside every day.

Every week, I get my paycheque. It comes in an envelope, along with a note. One hundred dollars, the cheque reads, stamped with a large VOID across the front. Attached to the cheque is a note, breaking down my earnings and expenses.

Paid labour: $100, it reads.

I look down.

Housing: $100.

Food: $50.

Round-trip Transportation to Job Site: $35.

Uniform, Cleaning and Equipment Replacement Fund: $10

Doctor Visit: $15

Total Expenses: $210

Total Earning: $100

Employee owes Construction Company $110. Paycheque withheld, interest-free loan extended. Thank you for being a valuable member of our team.

It's the same every week.

At the bottom, I see the total amount that I owe before I can quit and return to Pakistan: $46,288. Every week I owe them more for the work I do. Every week I am further away from ever seeing my family again.

Once a year, at the start of Ramadan, the company gives us a phone card to call our families back home. The men here come from all over SE Asia and the Middle East, but most of us from Pakistan. We get $20, enough to buy 100 minutes. Of course, that gets tacked right back onto our bill.

Sometimes, I see men tumble from the towers, after a misstep, and I wish I could do the same. But, it is not Allah's will. I still have work to do, I guess, so I sleep in shifts. I work and I pray. I have faith that one day this will all be over. If not in this life, I will be rewarded in death.

And I toss rocks.

Chink. Chink. Chink.

Sometimes, I get the angle just right, and in the light

of the moon, I can see them skip and skid across the floor like they did when I was a boy, standing in the stream with my brothers. And I close my eyes and feel free.

Alana Garrigues is generally a journalist and creative nonfiction writer who is dipping her feet in fiction with Moonlit Memories in this anthology. She was first exposed to the ugly truth about modern slavery and human trafficking during a visit with a United States Senator in college, and has followed the stories of these silent men, women and children ever since.

Alana sits on the board for Build a Better Benin, a non-profit organisation dedicated to improving the lives of women and children in West Africa, several touched by forced marriage or human trafficking. She is currently working on a full-length "humorous humanitarian" account of the BABB founder's life in the bush.

Originally from the bookish mecca of Portland, Oregon, she now lives the eternal sunshine life in Redondo Beach, California with her husband and identical twin daughters. Alana is an avid traveller, meticulous researcher, terrible housecleaner, red pen addict, incessant daydreamer, nature lover, and dabbler in all things art related.

She is also the Publications Editor for CBW-LA where she co-edits and contributes to the annual Writing Day *Story Sprouts Anthology*, and author of the writercize blog, home of original writing prompts for writers, students and teachers.

Alana loves the power of the written word to educate, to inform, to entertain, to inspire and to set free.

Visit alanagarrigues.com for more information.

INSURRECTION

BY KL MABBS

I clutched my mother's letters to my breast, hoping they would give me the courage I needed. How would I know if the pale things I called emotion could even resemble something like bravery. It's like walking into the blade of a combine to save a child. How could one do it? Faith isn't the answer. I don't believe in God, nor, I'm sure, do the Idran.

I stepped into the hospital where I would take the first step to kill the Idran and their Anasi. The consequences though, would that be for me alone, or humanity?

oooOooo

My dearest daughter, Rachael:

The Idra. They came to our world so gently, and we were happy to meet them. They came down from the sky, in each hemisphere, when the sun was shining, like an omen of doves wreathed in laurel. The people of the world took it that way, at least. Humans shouted out their admiration, an exhilaration that filled the bright air in every major city.

The universe wasn't lonely any more.

The Idran name sounds so innocuous, like a good Italian family name. You won't know Italy in your time, but in mine, it was a country of glorious treasures. The center of a spiritual nation. The Idra don't have religion, just their damn Anasi: their emotional constructs. A pool of sentiment that shrouded their feet in shadow. How had they ever learned to separate their emotions in such a manner? I shuddered at the thought. It's abhorrent. With the power they projected, it's no wonder we were happy. They made us feel... it was like having a sociopath come for dinner, smiling in all the right places. And most of us, unaware.

I am so proud of you, Rachel. That you will be able to read and understand these letters one day is a certainty to me. But to feel them, if you can—to know the tears we've all shed—that is my true desire for you. They've taken so much from us. From you. I am unsure if you are aware of this, but my heart holds you close. Remember, always, you offered us the hope for a future: in your words and deeds, and your idea that we could defeat the Idra.

oooOooo

The medical office was a place of textures. Supple flooring under my feet, pleasing shapes coming from the walls, and the colours—soft blues and greens designed to sooth. An ocean of peace. A false breath. I held mine, once again.

Equipment and furniture rose from the floor as needed. Ship tech: theirs. My apprehension, such as I could feel, climbed, even though I had been here before.

I had thought my shaking hands would have given us away, my child and me, that first day. But, the Anasi hadn't noticed the emotions; the gene therapy my child carried, and the Idra's arrogance, masked us.

"Private Rachael, what can I do for you today?" Sam said, from under thick salt and pepper quills, almost looking like hair, slicked back, hanging just past his shoulders. Fear would make them stand on end. Enough fright and they would explode outward. Atavistic racial protection they no longer needed. An elephant with claws.

"I'm fine," I said.

The room smelt clean, like antiseptic, but it didn't come from the sterile walls. It oozed from the Idra in front of me. Like venom from the golden skin of a poison dart frog.

His uniform blues were crisp in texture, and the bright colour made his gray-tinged skin look washed out. The lieutenant bars on his sleeves offered a dignity I had never been able to find in his face and form. To his credit, he was always kind. They all were. I'm sure that was part of their genetic programming. Their one constant.

It took concentration to remind myself that they were the enemy.

ooOOoo

Rachael:

I was so young when the Idran first came.

They kept us in warehouses—one, ten, or a thousand—we didn't know how many. Inside those buildings, we felt an ache for our freedom, rebelliousness, covered over by their projected happiness. Outside, for those of us that found the thought to leave, an oppression of misery fell upon us so fierce that we fell to our knees in subjugation. Some of us though, could handle that oppression.

And misery loves company.

I didn't breed with them willingly, nor did some of the others; we also weren't physically capable, not at first. But, they changed us. And then they made us want them... I remember touching them with a caress as soft as starlight, at the same time as the tears flowed down my cheeks, the Anasi urging every touch I gave. They didn't stop at one urging, or ten. All of us felt it for months. They called it 'readiness'. How does one get ready for a breeding program? Lick their master's hand?

When I was pregnant with you, Rachael, I promised I would find a way to escape.

I watched them from under downturned eyes, brief glances to keep their suspicions away. Compliance to keep their emotional constructs away. It wasn't easy but we had numbers on our side, groups of humans that refused to succumb, and we had power that way. A means to communicate, the chime of a cup against a metal railing.

The Idran missed the small things, a kitchen knife— there were so many uses for that—a weapon, a scraper, to loosen mortar from the bricks of a wall. A fork became a lock pick. One bed sheet out of a hundred became rope, bandages, or twine. We talked, and we were careful.

We would only get one chance.

We ran, hiding from the Anasi. Finding their range of influence, we were always wary. But hunger can make one careless. They found me one day, foraging, away from the group. My heart raced, fast enough to stutter even, but they passed me over for one of those not changed; unlike the dozen of us that had escaped the Idran. Even then, in my womb you were teaching me. We knew they had changed us. It was something we felt anew in our womb, a fear that spread with each trimester. All the women like me earned that knowledge, but that was our first lesson.

We learned to dampen what we felt, to keep them from sensing us.

They used emotion as Machiavelli used pain, projected it like a whip, to pierce the skin above our hearts and shrive our minds, to play the weaker of us against each other. One more weapon, though, the Idran added. They gave their shadows, the Anasi, an icon form. One of our own symbols, the Caduceus, without the separation of the staff or it's healing grace. It was an Archetype, atavistic and primal. The Anasi, as serpents, would wing after us, seek us out as before, but our hindbrains were screaming now, gibbering like some primitive life form on the run.

ooOOoo

The Idran had raped me—considering how they muted my emotions from birth, it was a wonder I even screamed, but I did.

I didn't even think it would lead to childbirth.

That was their cycle, though. It was how my mother came to bear me and how we came to find a solution: within our genetic changes.

The ancient physician, Asclepius had said, "Do no harm". But that was before the enemy had usurped our race and changed our structure, the way some wasps birth their young, taking over a spider, changing its will and its web.

I took a seat; the chair sprang to life. Sensors hummed as they came online, an automatic response to the weight of my body. The couch calmed emotions, reacting to physiological functions, even if they were mine. The chair's vapour skin analysed sweat and pheromones for abnormalities. Sound harmonics reduced stress. This was fighter tech, ours, from before the invasion. The Idra could have used the Anasi as emotional sensors, but that took energy. They thought us tame enough to forego the expenditure.

"It's my child. I think something is wrong." The lies flowed easy enough, now. The chair had quietly worked overtime that first day, my muted emotions running askance, like a broken trust. I had kept shaking, under my skin where I imagined my soul lay hidden and unaffected by their genetic manipulation. The emotions came in fits, and when I left, the nausea... it almost gave us away. I was so sure it would. But, I had gained their confidence. Somehow.

"Our children are very hearty, Rachel?" Sam said. They took our names, to make us more comfortable. His voice was a soft murmur like a shout underwater. His pronoun usage made the bile in my stomach want to overflow. It wasn't the first time he had said it that way, 'our child', but the Idran took things. It was their nature.

On the wall in front of me, his Anasi ranged back and forth. Shaped like the Caduceus: an icon they had stolen from us for their emotional shadow. They used these dual serpents to sway our minds and that part of our brains that didn't understand, but just ran with fear. As far and as fast as possible. But humans fight; that's our nature.

Our Shamans, the wise men of the *Nuu-chah-nulth,* thought the Anasi evolved enough to be genetic symbiotes. The way they moved in response to the Idran, the passion that grew in their eyes; these were things that were noticeable. When we had time to look. Two separate entities connected, Idran and Anasi: intellect and emotion.

It had been disconcerting the first time I'd seen the serpents. Their eyes were too sharp, as if searching for a mate's intimacy. Their wings too brilliant. One name only, for all of them. The upper echelon of the enemy held them, these totems of the soul. The emotions split from the Idran gene structure and given mobility. Their constant.

Host and larvae.

oooOooo

My child:

You grew so fast. I can't believe it. Your long dark hair, like corn-rolls, but I had never braided them. Your eyes were so stark, a grey as wide as a lemming's, with the truth of another species shining there. You were standing in months, and walking—the muscles of your arms and legs were so strong. And baby fat, it just wasn't there. But you didn't need to worry about a fall; the armour they gave you was protection enough. I was glad for it when you first started climbing trees.

oooOooo

My Love:

Those first words you said to me; 'What am I'? They spoke of so much, but mostly, they told me that you saw your differences, compared to us: your community, and to me, your parent. But that taught us to look closer, too. To see how the Idran had changed us. To ask what it meant. How we could fight them, our enemy. And when you understood, you told us. Use their emotions against them. Turn the Anasi against the host.

I have loved you so much and even though your responses are muted, almost clinical, I have to believe that you love me too. Because you touch me, for no reason. Or you would come in from an activity to watch me, and assure yourself I was there. What else could it mean?

It has taken so long to find a haven. A place where we could grow, not only for you but also for us, so we could counter what the Idra have been doing. The Nuu-chah-nulth became our tribe. They run and hide better than we ever had, and yet, they are organised. Each place and dwelling we reside in had the means to let us continue to grow, to learn about our enemy. The knowledge we have is no longer being lost. Better yet, the Anasi are at bay because of the Shaman's skills.

oooOooo

I folded the cloth of my uniform between thumb and forefinger, my hard nut-brown skin a rich contrast to the green material. I wasn't a Shaman or a Priest, just a soldier, but my recent vision—the Shaman's said we would know the time—was the reason for this visit to the medical office.

oooOooo

My child, children within me—I didn't know which—had jumped at the vision's intrusion.

The air had wavered, thickened, and fingers appeared. Tiny hands pulled at the angora bedspread, made a gentle fist, and then unclasped. Small toes formed at the other end, half curved in a stretch.

In the crib, the vision infant's skin shaded into being, the gentle features of the face appeared. Hair grew and thickened as if from nothing. The eyes blinked open. The child looked at me, awareness coming with the rest of the body, his blue eyes bright as

53

a cobalt bomb.

I reached out and caressed his fine black hair. The child responded and raised his head to stare directly at me.

I watched a second body slowly form beside the first vision child, the outer edges of the body first, and then the bulk coming last. The girl's emerald eyes pierced mine and held them for the attention she deserved. So much awareness. Her large pupils questing everywhere. Black hair, like twisted quills, so much like my own.

ooOOoo

"I'm scared—for my child, Sam." Another lie. The life within me is sustenance, a pool of water in a barren sietch. We had to be here. Today. My baby was old enough and the gene therapy was aggressive, now. I hoped. The chair settled, taking away some of my apprehension.

"Ah. Let's run some tests then." He put a stethoscope to the depression where his ears should have been and then warmed the diaphragm in his hands. They had four fingers and an opposable thumb, like us. So much like us. I'd always thought it odd he didn't use his own medtech for this. They liked the murmur of a heartbeat—so like a wave of sunlight coursing through space.

"You believe me?"

"Of course, Rachael. We take care of our own." There it was again, that pronoun. This time I held the bile in the back of my throat, swallowing before the acid could burn too much.

We worked their factories, and labs. We did their wet-work for them. That was what they meant by 'own'. Just another possession.

He made a motion with his hands near the buttons of his shirt. I loosened my dress greens for him. The diaphragm in his hands was too warm. I didn't flinch at his touch this time. I wouldn't have to feel his fingers against my flesh again, as if feeling a spider creep over one's hand.

I watched him listen, his indigo coloured eyes intent. Behind him, the serpents were just as studious. It was odd for a representation to have so much... presence. But, that's why we were here. My child and I.

"And the Anasi? What are they?" The serpents looked at me—their stare too much like the children's gaze from my vision. I shuddered as the image came back to me.

Our Shamans said we would know the right time. Did the others get the vision? A thousand pregnant woman, a thousand Idran and their Anasi.

"The Anasi are part of us, Rachael, but too separate. That will change, though." He almost smiled, as if he told a joke. The Idran didn't understand humour, though.

I didn't understand his meaning, either. Maybe it was the fear I was feeling. I would have been incapacitated had I felt the full fury of that emotion.

Yes. Like my ancestors had felt when they first met the Anasi.

The Idran had forced the Anasi on the resistant humans. On the religious that had faith and believed in salvation. The arrogant.

Some of the races of earth didn't succumb fast enough.

Thirty years ago, the Idra came to earth. *Told us what to feel.* Got my mother pregnant. Made us all become what they needed, emotionally, physically. The Islamic didn't understand that. They thought their faith would solve the oppression. They believed God would lift their spirits. They prayed, revolted, and put the righteousness of God into their hearts and arms. Their rifles spat the breath of God.

Death to the infidels.

The Idra pounded them into the ground with their own emotion of righteous fury. God had teeth. And the Islamic were humbled unto death. Their scripture destroyed.

The Chinese followed. They wanted to be social. To act under a sincere nature. But they were really reacting, trying to save their people before the Idran's had a chance to know what the left hand was doing. Dealing with the monsters under contract negotiation was a deception. Buddha became a shamed God under the influence of the Anasi. The Chinese were crippled in their numbers. The shame bursting their hearts in a flow of blood and tears that lasted for days. After that, the governments of humanity grew pale, shaken as salt.

Our Shamans though, men of spirit and science, took a different view, a longer perspective.

oooOooo

Dearest:

You learned how to read and write, years ago, but I never saw you use those skills beyond gaining knowledge, certainly not to read for pleasure. You can imagine my surprise when I found you listening to the stories of the Shamans. The ones that told of their past. The Great Wheel, the Sacred Numbers, the Coyote that taught lessons of deception. Oh, I knew they had knowledge in them, but it was the emotions they told, and your rapt attention to those details that astounded me. Drove the breath from my body at your receptiveness.

oooOooo

He held another instrument and put it over my arm. I knew from previous tests it examined my blood. The device wasn't their tech. It was Chinese: lost knowledge, until they learned to reverse engineer it.

Sam reached for yet another tool. One I hadn't seen before; Idran, I was sure. A butterfly rose out of the bile in my stomach, its wings caught in my throat. The tool fit over the curve of my stomach. A holo-interface sprang to life at his touch. The chair beneath me hummed in response to my newest surge of emotion. Why this sensitivity? Why now?

"Let's see if this child is ready."

Why did he say it that way? I tried to calm myself. The chair hummed again, responding to my stress. The Idran breeding program for humans had gotten us all used to the armour hard skin and the night vision. We fought their wars for them. They made good soldiers out of us. Could he see the new gene the Shamans had infused with my child?

"There. Everything's fine. Good soldier material. It's..."

"...No! I still want the mystery." I held my hands out trying to stop his voice. His quills shook. I smiled at his reaction; his simple response calming me more than the chair had. The Idra didn't understand parental anticipation.

We didn't even know how they had children. Yes, they raped us, but we were still human, even me. What would their children look like? Or even—were they loved?

The Anasi fluttered over the walls and then twined together. All they needed was a staff thrust between them for the transformation to begin, like that old story of Tiresias the Seer.

Our children—a thousand Trojan horses—were that staff. One thousand strong. We had timed this, like a virus with a built-in clock. The others: were their visions the same as mine had been? Did they even get the warning signal?

The Anasi lifted its twin heads off the wall, separating from their host in a way that couldn't have been possible before this. As real as the Anasi were, they had always been a two-dimensional construct.

The Idra followed my gaze. His shoulders tensed, his quills flared, and pain crossed his soft features. He spoke one last time, a whisper I barely heard. "That's the way. Thank you, Rachael, for the..."

I was sure he was wrong.

I'd heard the words, but still... I didn't understand. Didn't want to know.

We were revolting, taking back our lives. But, there was no fear in his eyes. His quills reacted, but I didn't know what the emotion was, couldn't understand the look on his face or the words he had spoken.

"...for the grandchildren." *He was happy with my choices*!

We didn't know, none of us.

The Anasi moved again, this time towards my child, seeking the stronger host. Their wings were coherent light. Brilliant. Their eyes—azure blue and emerald green—flared with understanding. The pain they should have felt from their separation from the Idran was lost in seeking the new therapy we carried.

Joining with my child.

oooOooo

My dearest Rachael:

I love you, I do. That is why I am staying behind this time. The Shamans have found a way to implement your ideas and they need time, as you do, to fit into the Idran enclave. I'm so proud of your bravery. Your choices. To grow up and become the soldier you are. The soldier they would want back. We've had the clues before us all this time, in you, and the others like you.

The Anasi found this enclave, but it is the least of the many that we own with our brethren. And they had to find us, so you could return to the Idra freely with no suspicion on their part.

Without emotions, Sam's quills died, flattened to his head. His bluish-purple eyes faded to lilac as he sank to the floor. He wouldn't survive the recombination, with his soul ripped from his psyche—I sighed. The smell in the room changed. The hot pepper stench of his urine filled my nostrils.

My children kicked as I left the Med Center. Twins. I knew it, now, as their awareness flooded through me. One with cobalt blue eyes and one with emerald green.

I rubbed my hand over the offspring within my womb and thought of the love I felt for them. It washed back over me like cherry blossoms let loose on a windy spring day.

I was so sure that was a good thing.

KL Mabbs grew up in Vancouver, BC, Canada, wanting to write about heroes the way Robert E. Howard did, or Edgar Rice Burroughs. The original inspiration for his hero worship was his parents, who saved the whole family from a fire.

Nowadays he writes with passion and emotion to make heroes like his parents come to life; stiff competition for any fantasy hero.

He has a fantasy book, *Spellsword*, coming out with Fey Publishing this year (2014), and is self-published on Amazon, with *Wolf: A Military P.A.C. Novel* (2012) military sci-fi and the *God'less Saga*, (2014) also military sci-fi.

Look for more from Mr. Mabbs at http://klmabbs.com.

THE RIGHT THING

BY CADDY ROWLAND

Feeling the contents of his breakfast threatening to come up, Brian pushed away from the table and hurried to the bathroom. He made it just in time. Heaving into the toilet bowl, he waited until certain his stomach had emptied.

When it seemed safe to do so, he flushed the toilet, stumbling to the sink to brush his teeth and gargle. He carefully avoided his reflection in the mirror.

I didn't know. I didn't know. This mantra repeated in his head, but no matter how often he thought those words they didn't become any more believable.

At last he allowed himself to look. Guilt. It was written all over his face. *Do the right thing, you son of a bitch. You have to do the right thing.*

Brian, a typical middle-aged man, had a wife and a couple of kids. He held a white collar job in middle management. His oldest was a boy, Robbie, who had just turned sixteen. The youngest, Melissa, had just turned twelve. His daughter. His princess.

Like most married couples, sex had waned when the children came. Although he loved his wife, Mandy, that most intimate part of the husband/wife relationship had never gotten back to the wild, uninhibited type of sex they had enjoyed before having a family.

Still, he knew they had a better sex life than many of his friends. Even so, it hadn't been enough. Brian wanted more; felt he deserved better. He worked hard all day and still had an appetite for great sex. Why couldn't his wife put in full days as a teacher and come home with libido intact?

If pushed, he would admit she did a lot more than teach. She cooked dinner, drove the kids around (thank God Robbie now had a license and a used car), and did most of the cleaning. Because she did so much, he always felt guilty even thinking about expecting her to play the part of a wanton sex goddess. He let her be, pretending to settle for a weekly quick screw, usually in the missionary position, as quiet as possible so the kids wouldn't hear.

She was interesting, fun, and kind. He was still crazy for her, which was why he started doing what he did. He convinced himself he was actually doing his wife a favour by electing to use a prostitute a couple of times per month.

oooOooo

It had started out as a promise to himself that it would only be one time—just to see how it felt to have dirty sex with a whore. What man didn't dream of a woman who would do exactly as he commanded? Even better, after being sated he could simply leave and get on with his night.

One time turned into a couple of times a month. Then, as his income rose, he got into the habit of using whores weekly.

It was so easy! He had seen the ads on Craigslist. All sorts of women were featured, promising all kinds of things. Best of all, they looked young and full of energy. He could picture any one of them bending to do his will, never tiring of his requests. Dancing, stripping, anal, oral... he could have it all with no complaint. A couple of times if he was able to get it up more than once.

From the beginning, Brian often wondered where the girls came from. He'd seen TV programs on the news about sex trafficking, which had horrified him. How could those perverts use girls who averaged the same age as his Melissa? His heart thudded in his chest just thinking about a man using his princess in those perverse ways. More and more, it also seemed there were articles in magazines and newspapers about sex rings and abduction rings being busted. The dirty bastards. He hoped they rotted in prison.

If he looked carefully at the girls he used, it was hard to tell exactly how young they were. Yeah, they looked young—but every one of them assured him they were eighteen, nineteen... and who was he to doubt them?

Plus, they seemed to really enjoy it. If two people giving each other pleasure was wrong, what could be right?

The possibility continued to nag at him that he was using under-aged girls. Make-up could hide a lot. The pimp could pay for implants. Some girls developed early. He could be just as guilty as the men he reviled.

When he couldn't get rid of the growing fear that he was indeed using minors, he decided they were runaways who came from bad homes. While it didn't make prostitution right, they probably had it a lot better now. If they were minors, they had to be very close to legal age. This wasn't New York. It was Moorhead, Minnesota. Not exactly the hub of all things evil.

His latest trick was a petite blonde girl named Yvette. Her huge brown eyes were only dwarfed by the impossibly large boobs she sported on her chest. They couldn't be real, but they sure were fun to play with. Yvette had a small scar on her left cheek. It was shaped almost like a heart. Above it was a small mole. She called it her beauty mark.

With her youthful face and limber body, Brian began to doubt even more if the girl could be anywhere close to eighteen. She looked more like his daughter's age, with a lot more knowledge in her eyes and street talk on her lips.

But, damn, she had talent like no other between the sheets. He pushed the age question to the back of his mind. After all, he wasn't hurting anybody. She needed the money, and he needed the excitement. It was a win-win situation for both parties.

Until this morning.

II

This morning his daughter had cheerfully called Brian to the kitchen, excited that she'd gotten breakfast ready for her father. With Mom out of town, she decided to pamper him. He usually got his own breakfast ready, but she looked so proud holding out the chair for him that he couldn't tell her not to bother.

He'd set up the coffee the night before, timed to turn on thirty minutes before he'd need it. All she'd had to do was put some toast in the toaster, jelly on the table, cereal in a bowl, and add some milk. She probably felt like a celebrity chef, and he made certain to convince her of the fact.

Smiling up at her, he asked, "Sweetheart, would you mind bringing me the milk from the fridge? I'd like a little more on my cereal."

That's when it happened. In just a few seconds, Brian's world imploded.

She'd brought him the milk before answering the phone. It was one of her friends, and she immediately forgot about him in the frenzy of discussing what colour jeans she and her friends should be wearing today at school.

Polishing off his toast and slurping the last of his cereal from the bowl, Brian casually read the milk carton. Turning it around, he saw the picture of a girl, now aged thirteen, who'd been missing for a year. Her name was Josie Benjamin.

She was brown-haired, but looked surprisingly familiar. Then he noticed the small, heart-shaped scar on her left cheek. Above it was a mole.

ooOOoo

Brian continued to stare into the mirror. What kind of a sick reprobate was he? *My God, my God, it could be my daughter!* The information on the carton had stated the girl had been taken on a Saturday afternoon at a neighbourhood mall in Sacramento, California. How often did Melissa take a bus to meet up with girlfriends at their own shopping mall?

"Daddy, I'm leaving now!" called Melissa as she knocked on the door.

"Okay, princess," he managed to croak, trying for normalcy but not quite succeeding.

"Are you okay?" Her concerned voice was like a switchblade to the heart.

"Yes. Just feeling a little under the weather. There's something going around the office."

"No hug then?"

"No hug, princess. I don't want to make you sick."

Her happy laugh filled him with more shame than he could ever imagine existing.

"Okay, Daddy. See you later. I love you."

Swallowing the lump in his throat, he managed to answer, "I love you, too, sweetie."

After she left, he continued to stand at the sink, thinking. He wanted to report seeing the girl. He really did. It would be the right thing to do. If his daughter went missing, he and Mandy would be almost insane wondering where she was and what had happened. He knew they'd spend the rest of their lives hoping someone would report seeing her alive, somehow getting her back home where she could once again be loved and cherished.

But if he reported her, he would be exposed. He would lose everything: his wife, his daughter, the house, the career. His status in the community would go from admiration to derision and disgust. He might as well die.

And Mandy! What would it do to her? She'd have to move in order to get away from the gossip. Melissa and Robbie would be uprooted. They would all hate him. They'd all wish him dead.

No, it was too risky.

An idea came to him. There were still a few pay phones around. He'd seen some just the other day in the lobby of a hotel where they'd had a business meeting. He could go to that hotel and report seeing her. He'd be able to do the right thing and not lose his world.

Brain quickly called into work, telling them he'd be a few minutes late. Carefully writing down all the information from the carton he thought he might need, he left the house.

oooOooo

When he got to the hotel, he noticed the packed front lobby. A convention must be in town. That made it all the more unlikely he'd even be noticed. Brian knew he was worrying too much, but couldn't help being cautious. No sense taking chances.

When he got to the phones, he dialed the number he'd written down.

"Hello. I saw Josie Benjamin on the back of a milk carton. I know where she is." Fumbling in his wallet for the Craigslist ad, he continued, "She's in Moorhead, Minnesota. Call this number and say you want an evening with Yvette. That's her. Make it convincing or they'll know something's up."

He listened for a minute. "Yes, that's right. The number is right. Yvette. No, I want to remain anonymous. I guarantee this girl is her. Please hurry. I don't want her to be shipped off somewhere else before someone gets to her. They, um, well... they move the girls around every few months or so."

ooOOoo

Later that night on the news, a special report came on about a thirteen-year-old girl who had been rescued at the Big Bargain Inn on Interstate 94 in Moorhead. The reporter went on to say that she'd been trafficked into prostitution, but had been rescued by an anonymous man who had called in the information. "We believe it was because he'd been a customer that he recognised her. Thank God he decided to do the right thing."

Brian's arm reached out to hug Melissa to him. Mandy, looking furious, snapped, "What kind of animal uses a young girl for sex? His balls should be cut off!" Tears in her eyes, she looked at Brian. "He had to know, Brian. How could anyone look at her and not know she was just a kid?"

Willing his arms and legs not to shake, Brian simply said, "Well, at least he did the right thing. Maybe it was a wake-up call for him. We'll never know."

"Ha! I doubt it. Perverts seldom change. I hope he burns in hell."

Melissa shivered. "Me, too, Mom. I hope the puke burns in hell, too."

He doesn't have to, thought Brian. He's living in it right this moment.

Caddy Rowland is the author of *There Was a House*, a continuing saga of revenge and redemption about five girls and one boy who are sex trafficked. She also has a five book historical family saga called *The Gastien Series*. This story is about struggle and the quest for power, abuse of power, class discrimination, and achievement of dreams, and the cost of living life your own way. Her fiction is for adults, with adult themes and graphic scenes.

She grew up with a stack of books that almost reached the ceiling before she was five. Books, along with her vivid imagination, have always been some of her closest friends. Caddy lives with her husband, who was her high school sweetheart. They are owned by two parrots. Besides being a writer, she is an artist. One can often find her "makin' love to the colour" (painting) with loud music blaring. However, when writing she prefers silence or classical music. That way she can hear the characters telling the story. Her goal as an author is to make readers laugh, cry, think, and become intimately connected with her main characters. Connect with Caddy and her books at www.caddyrowlandblog.blogspot.com.

SLAVE TO FASHION

BY DESIREE NICOLE

"Oh my, Katha, that dress is magnificent. All your hard work has paid off!"

"Thank you, Parilla. It was difficult to get all the materials together for the slaves, but it was worth it," she said with a laugh. "Zura, would you please give it a spin? I want my friend here to see this dress in action."

Parilla let out a giggle. "I have tickets for the runway show."

"Yes, but this way you get to see it up close and personal." Katha winked. "Twirl now, Zura! I won't ask you again!"

The young woman standing in front of them gritted her teeth but obeyed. If Zura didn't obey, the collar around her neck would emit an electrical pulse. It was the way they kept her kind in line.

"It's so bright and shimmery!" Parilla said. "You've really outdone yourself this time. I'm jealous that this girl gets the honour of wearing it before anyone else!"

"Tell her thank you, dear." Katha spoke without so much as looking at Zura.

"Thank you, ma'am." The response was automatic.

Parilla gasped and clasped her hands underneath her chin. "She's such an obedient slave. You don't often find that in these young ones."

"I wouldn't have just any slave!" she said proudly.

"If you think about it, she's a slave to fashion." Parilla giggled.

Katha joined her in the laughter. "A slave to fashion? My, you are witty, Parilla!"

It was a nauseating response, but Zura held back her disgust. She showed it only briefly when her mistress's friend spoke again.

"You flatter me!" Parilla's cheeks were flushed. This made it clear she truly was flattered.

"Enough talk of such things, Parilla! We have a show to prepare for, and you have to get to your seat!"

Zura watched Katha and her friend walk behind the mirror. When they were out of the room, she sneered at the dress and dug her fingernails into her palms.

The girl beside her laughed. "They've done me up in a feather dress. I'd much rather be wearing what you have on."

Zura didn't laugh and instead frowned. "I don't know why one of those so-called fashion moguls had to buy me in the first place. I would rather be on a field, working in the hot sun, than playing dress up for that woman."

She watched as the look on the other slave's face turned from amusement to rage. It caused Zura to take a step back.

"We can complain about it all we want, but this life is certainly better then working on a field!"

Zura opened her mouth to respond but closed it when her mistress came back in.

"Let's go, Zura. You're going on in two minutes and then you only have five minutes to change into the next outfit," Katha ordered.

"Yes, mistress."

The fashion show was a blur for Zura. She had people poking and prodding her in the back rooms and then everyone staring at her while she was walking down the runway. After it was over, Zura had never been happier to be wearing her plain, simple clothes.

"Are the dresses all packed, Zura?"

"Yes, mistress."

"I had better not find a wrinkle on them."

"I doubt a wrinkle would be the worst thing that could happen to those monstrosities." Zura winced after she realised what she had said. She had been known to have a mouth on her, but three years with Mistress Katha should've stripped her of that trait.

Katha stiffened. "What did you say?"

"I-I'm so sorry, Mistress. I don't know what came over me— "

Zura couldn't finish her sentence because pain had started to course through her body. After it ended, she collapsed onto the ground and tried to curl into herself, but Zura's mistress wouldn't allow it.

"How dare you speak to me like that after I was kind enough to buy you?" Katha screeched. "Do you realise how pampered you are compared to most of your kind? You should be grateful!"

"What should I be grateful for?" Zura spat. "I hope you don't mean I should be grateful for your kind enslaving all my people because that's sick even for you, Mistress."

"I told you to behave!"

Zura screamed as her collar sent another shock through her body. The second hit had her panting and nearly whimpering in pain, but she couldn't stop. Zura wanted her to hear these things.

"I guess I'm not such a good girl after all, am I?"

The third shock of the collar caused Zura to black out.

oooOooo

"Zura, what has gotten into you?"

When she woke up, she was back in her little room

at the manor. Above her, Marta was patting her brow with a cloth, and she looked displeased.

"Marta..."

She shook her head. "How could you do something so stupid, Zura? You nearly got yourself sold back to the auctioneers!"

"I don't know what came over me. It was like something snapped inside and once the words came out, I couldn't stop them."

"Well it's over and done with, child. You need to focus on healing because the sooner you heal, the quicker you can get back to work for our mistress," Marta assured her.

"So I'm just supposed to go back to being her dress up doll?" Zura spat. "I won't do it, Marta. I just won't."

Marta smiled sadly. "Sometimes we must do things we don't like. It is the way of the world."

"Do you remember before?" Zura was born and raised in slavery but had heard stories of life before Katha and her kind had come. It had always fascinated her.

"It was a lovely place, and while it wasn't perfect, it was home. I remember every year looking forward to the King's festival, and what a joyous occasion it was! There was singing, dancing, and all sorts of games." She spoke with an expression of fondness on her face. It only made Zura feel even bitterer.

"Then they came?" Zura asked

"Then they came." Marta's face filled with sadness. The joy and fondness for the past memories were no longer there.

"When I was small, I remembered the stories my mother used to tell me from when she was just a child. She said the only wish she had was that I get to see the way our land used to be."

Marta hushed her. "Enough talk of sad things, Zura. You need to rest before you get back to work."

She wanted to shout at the top of her lungs that it wasn't fair. It was an urge Zura shoved to the back of her mind as she settled on the cot. One look at Marta told her she should hurry and close her eyes.

It was only a few hours later when Zura woke. Marta was no longer present; she had probably gone back to work. The pain Zura had felt before was nearly gone when she finally stood. She only winced once.

A look out the window told her it was well into the evening. She had slept longer than she intended, but the rest had worked. When Zura walked into the hall she heard the sound of footsteps and chattering servants. One of the voices she recognised as Marta's.

She rushed over the second she spotted her. "Zura, you're awake finally! How do you feel?"

"I feel much better."

"Then back to work with you! You can start by putting away the rest of the clothes that our mistress brought to the fashion show." Marta patted her gently on the shoulder and then went on her way.

Zura left as soon as Marta faded from her sight. It was but a short walk to the storage room where the Mistress had the dresses. A good number of the dresses had been put away, but a few more remained. The one Zura had worn, the one with all the sequins, was hanging on one of the mannequins.

The sight of it made her stomach churn. Zura marched up to it and clutched the fabric of the horrid dress tightly in one of her hands. She gave it a firm tug and some of the sequins scattered onto the floor. It would only take a few more powerful tugs to rip the dress to shreds but something stopped Zura at the last second.

She fell back from the dress and clasped her hand over her mouth in order to muffle the sobs. If Zura tore the dress, it would bring her nothing but hardship. Many slaves weren't as lucky to be bought by someone of high status like she had been. They worked in factories, farms, or even in brothels where only suffering was known.

Zura wanted to rip the dress to shreds so badly. It

was a sign of her enslavement, but she wouldn't destroy it. She did have it easier than many other slaves, but it would never be enough.

For as long as she was a slave, nothing would ever be enough.

Even though she is a few years shy of thirty, Desiree Nicole has yet to learn the true meaning of the term adult. She resides in a small town in New York where she spends her time working, going to school, and trying to finish that pesky novel of hers.

This is her first published story.

PET PROJECT

BY REBECCA FREEMAN

Rhyso was in the food prep area when Deek came back from work. As Deek walked past the doorway, Rhyso was bent over something on the counter, and Deek remembered, with some regret, that it was the dinner party tonight. Perhaps Deek could pretend to be ill? Or tell him that Flio was ill? That would mean lying, though. And whatever one might accuse Rhyso of, he could spot a lie.

"I know you're thinking about trying to get out of tonight," Rhyso called, eyes still fixed on the food. "But I expect you there. No excuses."

"Flio isn't feeling too well," Deek said

"Pff. She's fine. I checked on her earlier. Still looks as miserable as ever."

Deek slid his files into the cabinet near his unit and pressed his print on the wall sensor to secure them.

"It's how she always looks," he sighed. "I checked the factbook. It says it's normal for yumas to look like that."

"Well, she looks sad to me. She made those noises again. Always the same noises, you know? I wonder what it means?"

"She's a pet, Rhyso. You can't use the same logic for them as you can for us. I just wish I could find out what she was thinking. I hate to think of her being unhappy."

"Well, she's your baby. Maybe you can get Visp to check her out. He's got a couple of yumas, hasn't he?"

Visp. He had five. He was always lauding it over the rest of them. Nobody was sure how he kept all of them; yumas weren't exactly cheap to feed, and it was hard finding the right care for them when they got sick. As far as Deek knew, there was only one specialist on the base, and she was expensive. If Flio was sick, Deek supposed he was better off asking Visp's advice, rather than having to wait for an appointment. He would rather not have to, though. Visp prided himself on his knowledge of yumas. Deek usually avoided the subject whenever they happened to run into each other.

"I'll go and check on her," Deek muttered. "Oh, and who else did you say was coming tonight?"

"Just a few others. The fleet is in from one of the near colonies, so I thought I should get the old crowd together before it gets too busy on base."

Deek stopped in the doorway to the basement.

"Tell me you didn't invite Prenliya."

"OK, sure, if it makes you feel better."

"You did invite her, didn't you?"

Rhyso raised his head from the food preparation.

"Deek, it's been four lunar-cycles. Surely you can stand to be in the same quarters together for a few hours. Besides, I thought you said you might think about seeing her colleague, so I invited him as well. What's his name?"

Deek cleared his throat.

"Elter."

This was getting worse by the second. His ex, his crush, and the most boring acquaintance he knew were all going to be in the same room. Life was unfair.

"I'll be downstairs checking on Flio. Let me know when they arrive."

He padded slowly down the stairs to the basement and flicked on the lights. Flio was huddled in her crate. Visp had mentioned that he'd bought outfits for his, so Deek had found a place which sold yuma clothing, and bought her some. He had only tried one outfit on her so far, and as much as he hated to admit it, Visp was right. She did seem to be a little more relaxed.

He took a scoop of food and walked over to her crate. She glanced at him, and returned her gaze to the floor in front of her. Perhaps there was something to what Rhyso was saying. She did seem to be a little sad. But how was he even supposed to know? The chattering she made was unintelligible, and as far as he could tell, this was simply the way that yumas behaved. Sometimes he wondered if he would have been better off getting a Centris worm. At least they were entertaining, if not exactly cuddly.

"Deek!"

Rhyso was calling him. He supposed the guests had arrived. Deek emptied the kibble into the dish in Flio's crate, and stretched out to pat her on the head. He'd had her clipped recently and the stubbly growth was soft under his touch. She looked at him, and made one of her chattering sounds.

He smiled at her and turned to go back up the stairs. He would come back and visit after the main course. Since Rhyso had already mentioned that she might be unwell, he could hardly object to Deek coming to check on her, and therefore getting some time away from the party.

He could hear Visp's voice in the entranceway as he reached the top of the stairs, and as he walked into the hall, Visp greeted him as if they were friends.

"Deek! Good to see you home so early! You've been spending so much time on deck I wondered if you were pulling overtime to save up for another yuma!"

Already on the topic of yumas, Deek thought. As if it were the only thing to talk about. Still, Visp had so many of them, he supposed there was little else that interested him.

"Oh, one's enough for me," Deek replied, forcing a smile.

"Oh, but the breeding! You don't want to breed them?"

Deek shook his head, and tried to catch Rhyso's eye, to see if they couldn't move the conversation onto something else.

"I'm getting another two females next lunar cycle," continued Visp, accepting a drink from Rhyso. "I'll put them with the males I already have and see what happens. It takes a while for them to warm up to one another, but leave them in a crate together for long enough, and they'll mate. One of my original females is already pregnant."

"Oh," said Deek, feeling a little uncomfortable with all this talk of mating and pregnancy. "And... uh... when do you expect she'll give birth to her young?"

Visp was about to answer when the door sensor signalled the arrival of more guests.

"I'll get that," called Deek, hurriedly, and rushed to let the others in, only realising as the door slid back, that Prenliya would likely be one of those standing on the threshold.

"Pren," Deek said.

"Hi Deek," she replied, and brushed past him.

The others nodded at Deek and he smiled as they filed past him. Rhyso was handing out drinks and beginning to recount the day's dramas in administration. He was a natural entertainer, and Deek hoped that the guests' attention would be so keenly focused on Rhyso, that Deek would be able to slip away for a few minutes and collect his emotions. But just as he was about to step into his own cubicle, Visp turned around.

"Deek! Come, I must tell you about the new catalogue I'm compiling..."

This time, Rhyso noticed Deek's expression and announced that the meal would be ready soon, and showed them into the dining area.

Once seated and eating, Deek felt a little better. The others knew each other well, so there were few awkward silences, and Rhyso's food was, as usual, superb. During a lull in the conversation, Visp held up his utensils and waved to get Deek's attention.

"We were interrupted before," he said, "when I was going to tell you about my catalogue."

"Ah. Yes."

Deek smiled politely.

"I'm making a catalogue of the different yuma breeds. You know how they come in different colours?"

Deek nodded.

"Well, I've heard that you can mix them, to get variations in the colour of the young! It's very exciting. So I want to start collating information about how to get the most interesting combination. It's going to take a while, of course, as their gestation period is quite long, but I think it will be really worth it. You might be interested in putting yours forward for mating, maybe?"

"Well... I'd not really thought of it—"

Deek began, but Prenliya interrupted.

"I think it's cruel," she said, looking from Visp to Deek and back again. "I've heard they're quite sentient. Keeping them in cages and breeding them... what do you even know about them and their habitat?"

Deek resisted the urge to roll his eyes. He knew that his understanding of yumas was limited, but Pren had just given Visp an excuse to demonstrate just how vast his knowledge was.

"Their home planet, Arrit, was one of our early conquests," Visp began, "and we recreate their atmosphere very well through the specialised yuma crates. As for the yumas themselves, they seem to be quite primitive. Some ability to use tools. No understanding of the deeper, more philosophical aspects of life, especially life beyond their own planet. Easily confused and sometimes hard to keep in captivity... they tend to mope and withdraw if not properly stimulated. You're really better off having more than one, I feel."

He looked meaningfully at Deek, who pretended to be interested in the last of his food.

"Well, I just can't see the point," insisted Prenliya. "Why keep them at all?"

"Why keep any pet?" laughed Visp. "They're interesting. After a while in captivity, they become less shy. They eat out of your hand and try to communicate. It's sweet."

"I can see where Prenliya is coming from."

Deek turned to see who had spoken, and realised it was Elter.

"Of course, their sentience is what appeals to us. And as Visp says, they're interesting. But possibly, we need to learn a bit more about where they come from before we keep them as pets. After all, that's the ethical question Prenliya is raising, isn't it?"

Visp shook his head.

"No, no," he said. "I think we dealt with all the ethical questions when we first began to bring them back from Arrit. They simply don't have the same needs as we do. Oh, the food and shelter, of course. And as I said, perhaps some companionship between one another. But let's face it, they just don't think in any deeply intelligent way."

"Well, I'm afraid I must respectfully disagree," Elter said. "I wrote a thesis on yumas twelve sun cycles ago, when we first discovered Arrit and began bringing them back. I studied them for nine lunar cycles. I think they show real intelligence. Possibly more than we realise. They seem to have language, social structure..."

Visp made a noise which sounded like much less respectful disagreement.

"On that note," Deek said, the potential confrontation already making him uncomfortable. "I'm afraid I must go and check on Flio."

He nodded at the guests and Rhyso, and took his

plate with him to the basement. Perhaps Flio would like some table scraps—he'd never tried her with them before, but maybe it would bring her out of her melancholy.

He flicked the lights on again and saw Flio lying down in her crate. His hearts began to beat faster as he thought of all the things that might be wrong, all the potential diseases she could have developed, which he had no idea how to treat. As he rushed over, she stirred, and sat up. He blew out the breath he had been holding. She had simply been asleep. What a fool he was, not even being able to see that.

Deek reached in to get her food bowl so that he could tip the scraps into it, and was just about to take it through the gate when she reached out and touched him.

Deek froze. He had bought Flio almost a full sun cycle ago, and she had never once touched him. It was always him reaching out to her. He held his breath, not sure what to do in response, and not wanting it to stop.

"She is trying to communicate," said a quiet voice behind him.

"What is she trying to say?" Deek asked softly, not wanting to turn to face Elter in case Flio let go.

"She is trying to tell you how she feels. Tell you how it feels in her crate."

"Why can't they talk?" Deek whispered.

Flio let him go, and her eyes began to drip with water.

"Oh, now what?"

Deek couldn't keep the exasperation from his voice, and Elter laughed, but not unkindly.

"She is showing her emotions, Deek. She is desperately sad."

"But what could she possibly want? She has everything. I visit her every day, usually several times. I have her groomed."

Elter sat on the floor next to Deek and looked at him.

"Deek, I want to tell you something, and I need you to keep it to yourself. Can you do that?"

Deek nodded.

"I've been researching yumas for years, as you know, and I'm currently preparing a report for the fleet commander. It's going to show that yumas are actually intelligent life forms, and what we're doing here by keeping them as pets... well, it's essentially abduction."

"But..!"

"I know," Elter touched Deek's shoulder. "The thought has always been that they were primitive, and that meant, we thought we could do what we wanted with them. But you know, Deek, they're living creatures, just like us. We've taken them from their home, and we keep them in cages. What kind of beings does that make us?"

Deek shifted uncomfortably.

"This report is going to cause ripples across our whole fleet, and our home planet. Hopefully it will lead to changes across our whole galaxy, even further. They have languages. They have culture. They're just like us. You think they don't talk, they don't understand, but they do. The name we give them even is a derivation of what some of them call themselves: humans."

"Humans," Deek tried out the word. "But surely... we're giving them a new life here. I heard their planet was overrun. It can't have been an easy life for them. Here, they don't have to worry. I provide all Flio needs..."

Elter nodded.

"You also provide a cage. And their life may not have been easy on their home planet, but it was home."

Deek felt an irritation at how uncomfortable this was making him feel, and Elter seemed to sense this, because he went on.

"You have been kind to Flio, the best way you know how, even though you're keeping her in captivity. Others..."

He paused, and Deek knew he was referring to Visp.

"Well," continued Elter, "let's just say that others have been less kind. Forcing them to mate, breeding them to see which traits their offspring exhibit... these are wonderful creatures, Deek. Of course they can be cruel or violent towards one another, just like we are. But they also have such capacity for love for one another, just like we do."

Deek was silent. He looked into Flio's eyes. Elter was right. There was a spark there. Why had he not seen it before?

"So what do I do?" he asked Elter.

"There is a group of us. We are hoping to organise to present evidence to the fleet commander and then onto the government. We want to pass a law so that it is illegal to keep yumas, and to return them to their home planet."

"But... won't that be difficult?"

"Oh, of course!" Elter laughed. "There are many who like to show their wealth by the number or kinds of yumas they have. They won't want to give them up. And it will also set a precedent for how we treat life on other conquered worlds, which will be something that the fleet will likely resist."

"Well, why do it, then? I mean, I understand that you want to protect the yumas, but can't we just make sure they're treated better? Set a limit to how many you can own?"

Elter shook his head.

"Even a luxurious prison is still a prison, Deek," he said. "And there will always be those who find a way to circumvent the law. The only way to stop them is to legislate. Then we can prosecute."

Deek swallowed. His eye blinked.

"I know you'd like to keep her, Deek. But think how you would feel if you were far from home, alone, with no friends or family? No-one to communicate with? No idea if you were going to see your planet or those you loved, ever again?"

"I understand. I do. I just... it was good to have

84

something else to focus on. Other than work."

Elter placed a paw on Deek's forearm.

"There are other things you can focus on. You can help me, and the others, to get them home again. The higher ground is always more difficult, but the view is wonderful."

Deek smiled and placed his paw on top of Elter's.

"When do we start?"

Rebecca Freeman lives on the south coast of Western Australia with her husband and their dog, their chicken, three cats and four children. In between gardening, cooking and many, many cups of tea, she writes an almost-weekly blog on philosophy, ethics and cultural norms at thisclimbingbean.wordpress.com. She is currently working on a novel, a children's book, and a chapbook of poetry called 'The Pretend Parent'.

SECOND STAR

BY JOHN BELDEN

"Captain, we are in position."

Gwendolyn Byrd looked up at the xenoship's main bridge viewscreen. The star's image sat precisely in the center of the astrogator's bubble.

"Continue heading straight, zero deviation, accelerate only on my command," she said, hoping the emotions of this moment wouldn't choke the authority out of her voice. Perhaps if she held on to the anger, that would keep her orders sharp.

At last. The hunt was nearly over. This search had consumed her entire Royal Navy career—longer, in fact: as a teen constantly visiting the Cardiff spaceport, as a prep and college Cadet and finally, as the Ensign who became certified for off-Earth flight in record time. At last, she had found the way back, to avenge her brothers, to save the children. To find him.

She took on this mission like a sacred obligation. After all, she was the only child to come back. And she had the only clue to find the others. "Second star to the right and straight on until morning," he had said, too cocksure to guess that anyone would escape to use those instructions against him.

But, second star from what? That was the puzzle that tortured her, and others who worked on the search, for years. The second half of the instruction was easier to guess: in ultralow orbit, once the mystery vector is determined from London's coordinates, bear directly east until the exact moment of dawn. Then the rift would open, or at least become visible due to the angle of the sun's rays, and within moments you were there.

Only one other ship ever found it, the craft that carried her rescuer. Cpt. Hook somehow managed to follow an energy trail, slipping his two-person shuttle through. Saving her had cost his first officer, Smee, his life and Hook his sanity. (So plagued by paranoia and hallucinations, it only took the ringing of an old-fashioned alarm clock to trigger his fatal heart attack.) Though he had found her, the shuttle's computer failed to store the coordinates. Pan's cryptic instruction was still all they had to go by.

The process of elimination—fixing on the second star to the right of each heavenly body visible in the English skies one by one—had been frustrating and fruitless. With each year that passed, the search grew more hopeless. Then young Mr. Barrie came through; his overactive imagination finally became a boon to His Majesty's forces. Once he presented the solution, she knew it was right. In her heart she felt it, but kept that feeling to herself. This could have been another dead end. Still, by this point any solution stated with confidence would be accepted by the chain of command. With swift approval, the mission—and fully-equipped xenoship—were hers.

The mission also gained urgency for two important reasons. First, children had been taken all over the world. The other space powers—the U.S., Russia,

China, Japan and India—seemed happy to defer to the U.K. on this (why risk their own ships?) but observed the mission closely.

Second, he came for her daughter. She almost didn't see his dark symbiote—what he called his "shadow"—scouting around the windows of her home. It had even managed to evade the notice of their sheepdog. She knew this wasn't a coincidence, knew it was personal. After all, he almost always took boys, not girls.

It was a fluke that circumstances had placed her in her brothers' room when they first encountered him. He elected to take her, hoping to use her as some form of governess to manage his captives. She was his second attempt at giving his lost boys a "mother"—the first, a Native American girl, turned out to be too much like one of the boys herself. Instead, he found better use for her as his willing lieutenant, helping him to...

Best not to think of that. To think of what he does to them. What he did to Michael and John.

To remember the horrors was also to remember that she had seen him. Seen what he was without his glamour, his disguise as the mythical Old English Peter Pan. It was plain that Neverland was not of her world. And neither was he.

A streak of orange across the viewscreen jolted her out of thought. Without even glancing at the readouts she shouted, "Engage, full ahead!"

As quickly as the rift became visible, it flashed around them, and then the HMX Darling (named for her father, hero of the Pirate Wars) emerged in an alien atmosphere.

Immediately she could hear the ringing, almost below her auditory threshold, but she had been listening for it. And on screen she could see it, charging straight for the ship. Only centimeters tall, the crystalline being had immense power. Pan had used it to coat her and her brothers with quantum particles that allowed them to travel shipless and undetectable by terrestrial scans. Flight sounds like fun, but the side effects? Just ask Cpt. Byrd's oncologist.

She felt sure it knew she was aboard, that it was coming for her. Even when it feigned friendship with the boys, it never liked her. Well, the feeling was mutual.

As she glanced down at energy readings, preparing to order a weapons lock on that crystal bitch, for the first time in years, Wendy had a very happy thought.

About John Belden

John Belden is a journalist and writer, originally from Arkansas, living in Indiana. His work can be seen in the anthologies "Idol Musings" and "Idol Meanderings," and in some small-town newspapers.